A FREE MAN ON SUNDAY

By the same author

CHRIS AND THE DRAGON

JOSH'S PANTHER

A FREE MAN ON SUNDAY

Fay Sampson

LONDON
VICTOR GOLLANCZ LTD
1987

The Manchester Rambler
Words and music by Ewan McColl
Reprinted by permission of Harmony Music Ltd

First published in Great Britain 1987
by Victor Gollancz Ltd
14 Henrietta Street, London WC2E 8QJ

British Library Cataloguing in Publication Data
Sampson, Fay
A free man on Sunday.
I. Title
823'.914[J] PZ7

ISBN 0-575-04114-5

Photoset in Great Britain
at The Spartan Press Ltd,
Lymington, Hants
and printed in Great Britain by
St Edmundsbury Press Ltd,
Bury St Edmunds

TO EDITH

Author's Note

On Sunday, April 24, 1932, a Mass Trespass took place on Kinder Scout. John Anderson, Benny Rothman, Tony Gillett, Jud Clyne and Dave Nussbaum were sentenced to periods of imprisonment ranging from six to two months. Woolfie Winnick led the Trespass. All the other characters in this book are fictitious.

The National Parks and Access to the Countryside Act was passed in 1949. The Peak District National Park was the first and largest national park in Britain.

My warmest thanks are due to Benny Rothman for reading the manuscript and for generously allowing me to take fictional liberties with his name as well as recording his historic role. My thanks, too, to all those who organised the reconstruction of the Trespass in 1982, to the former "Trespassers" who shared their memories with me, and to Ewan MacColl and Harmony Music Ltd for permission to quote from *The Manchester Rambler*. The song was, in fact, written several years after the Trespass. But it captures the spirit of the time so perfectly that not to have used it would have been to put accuracy before truth.

F.S.

Chapter 1

'Jailbird!' Jimmy Greenwood's fat face was leering at her. 'Your dad's in prison, isn't he?'

'He isn't! He isn't!'

'Yes, he is, then. It was in the *Exchange and Echo*! *Clifford Ramsden, millworker, jailed for six months*.'

Voices clamoured round Edith.

'My mum says he hit a man with a stick. Split his head open.'

'My mum says I'm not to play with you any more.'

'My dad says your dad's a Commie.'

'He isn't! He isn't! He didn't hit anyone!' Edie broke away from them. She started to run across the playground. They were all jeering and taunting her now. They wanted to make her cry. They wanted to see her run, out of the playground and back home to her mother. But she was a Ramsden. She stopped running. She made herself walk quite slowly, fighting back the tears.

'Jailbird! Jailbird!
Clifford Ramsden's a jailbird,'

they chorussed, falling into step behind her.

Edith stuck her chin in the air and chanted back the old rhyme.

'Sticks and stones may break my bones,
But names will never hurt me.'

There. She had almost reached safety now. The door of the girls' lavatories. Jimmy Greenwood couldn't follow her in there.

'My dad said if that gamekeeper had died, they'd have had to hang your dad.'

It was too much. With a sob, she darted inside and slammed the door. The bolt rammed home.

'Jailbird! Jailbird!
Clifford Ramsden's a jailbird.'

But they couldn't stay outside for ever shouting at her. Mrs Bamfylde was on duty, and she'd notice. Then there would be trouble. The voices grew quieter, edged away, stopped.

Edith sat there, with her knickers round her ankles. She was crying now, out of sight. It was not just tears running down her face. She was shaking all over. That meant she would have to come out in front of them with her eyes red and her face all blotchy.

"Jailbird", they had called him. Clifford Ramsden. Her dad, in prison. And now she sobbed louder than ever, because it was true.

Chapter 2

She had sat in the Derby Assize Court beside her mother and heard the judge sentence him.

Her father had been wearing his Sunday suit, and his hair had been slicked back with brilliantine, as though the wind had never ruffled it. He stood out from the six younger men around him. In the sheep-pen of a dock he was like one of those pillars of stone that farmers bring in off the moor to use for a gatepost, which stands on, tall and unweathered, even though it has its feet in the farmyard muck. Clifford Ramsden was a tall, square-shouldered man, ginger hair darkened now by the oil, and freckles dimmed by the softly-coloured light falling through stained-glass windows. But he belonged out of doors, anyone could see that; and Edith's soul had cried out because the judge in his wig, sitting up there on the bench, could shut him away in a narrow cell in a prison, behind bars, within high walls, for taking that Sunday walk upon the hills.

The judge spoke severely. 'Clifford Ramsden. This court finds you guilty of riotous assembly and assault. Have you anything to say before I sentence you? You are older than these other misguided young men. Are you not ashamed of the example you set?'

Her father had lifted his head then, and his voice rang firm and true.

'No, my lord. I never hurt anyone. And if I were a free man, I'd climb that mountain again tomorrow.'

'Then, Clifford Ramsden, for riotous assembly and assault I sentence you to six months' imprisonment.'

She could not believe it. Even though she and her mother had sat here for two whole days fearing this. No one had told the jury what it had really been like. With all those words, no one had made them feel the sun on their faces and the wind in their hair. That day was like a book that has never been opened. Like a buried treasure that people walk over without realising it. The lawyers had made it sound dirty, like a fight outside a pub on a Saturday night. Fists, sticks, broken heads. And it hadn't been like that. It hadn't! She knew, because she had been there.

Margaret Ramsden grabbed Edie's hand and hurried her out of the courtroom, down the wide steps with the pigeons flying away from them. She spoke furiously, hiding the hurt and shame inside her.

'I warned him! I told him this would happen!'

Chapter 3

One weekend in March had changed the safe, familiar pattern.

'Have you got your boots ready?'

There was always that breathless moment when she looked at her father's laughing eyes as he came in through the door, and hardly dared to believe him. Even though it was what she had been longing for all Saturday morning as she dusted the bedrooms and polished the brass door-knobs. Even though her sandwiches were cut and ready on the kitchen table. But she never knew for certain till her father came home from his last shift at the mill at half past eleven.

Every five minutes she had scanned the narrow strip of sky above the street, fearful of every wandering cloud. He would go rambling himself, come hail or hurricane. But he would not take her if the weather promised badly. She was so much younger than any of the others. She would not have been allowed to go at all if he had not been her father.

So she never knew till the last moment whether it would be Saturday afternoon shopping with her mother, trailing through town, looking in windows at things they could never buy, dragging the heavy bags of groceries home, or whether it would be the glorious freedom of the moors with her father, the rolling footpaths and the open sky and the songs they sang.

'I want to come,' her brother Bobby said loudly.

A flash of bitter jealousy seared through Edie. Not Bobby too. These few hours with her father were so precious, the only time when he and she could be alone together. Alone, because the straggling line of ramblers in front and behind were no more to Edie than a warm blanket of friendliness wrapping her round, like the sun on her back. What mattered was her father striding beside her, his hand big and strong over hers as he helped her across a beck or lifted her down from a stile. She couldn't bear to share him with Bobby.

Clifford Ramsden smiled down at his small son, crinkling his eyes kindly.

'Hold out your legs, then.'

Bobby stuck them out in front of his chair importantly.

'Got a tape measure, Mother?'

Maggie turned from the gas stove to her sewing box by the fireplace. Solemnly Clifford measured Bobby's leg.

'Thirty inches. And the stepping stones on Yellowslacks are thirty-six apart. You've a bit of growing to do yet.'

'But you said Edie could go.'

Edie held out her legs to her father, hugging her laughter. He measured from the top of her tartan skirt down to her ankle.

'Thirty-six inches exactly. And it's a big stride, even for her.'

She knew he hadn't measured the stepping stones. But his eyes met hers in a smile that would have been a wink if Bobby hadn't been watching. She loved him for that smile.

'You could lift me over!'

'That I'll not! Edie walks on her own two feet, and so will any lad of mine. Next year, maybe.' And he rumpled Bobby's hair.

Bobby's mouth settled into an obstinate line. He knew better than to argue further. For a moment Edie felt sorry for him. Now he'd have to trail round the shops with her mother. Just the two of them. She saw her father slide a threepenny bit across the table towards Maggie, and knew that it was to buy Bobby sweets. Even that didn't matter. There would be a bar of chocolate in her father's rucksack that they would share when the footpath had carried them to their goal, wherever that was.

'Have you got our snap, Edie? We'll be missing that bus.'

She held up the sandwich tin proudly and dropped it into the big canvas rucksack that he carried for both of them.

'You watch how far you're taking her,' said Maggie. 'She's only eleven. She's still a child, remember.'

This time, Clifford did wink at her.

'Aye, but she's a Ramsden. That's worth two of anyone else. Are you set?'

They ran down the street, hand in hand. There was never enough time on Saturday, but it was all they had. Those that were lucky enough to have a job were working in the mill or in tiny offices until quarter past eleven. When the hooters sounded across the town, it was like a chorus of ships celebrating the weekend.

The boys and girls of Oldway Chapel Youth Club were already on the bus — some of the boys in shorts, the girls in sensible skirts and flat shoes. They carried canvas rucksacks stuffed with sandwiches and pop, stout raincoats, spare jerseys and socks. It was a point of pride to fill their rucksacks as full as they could, as though they were going on a week's expedition. Tomorrow they would be in chapel together looking quite different, the boys in dark suits, the girls in their best coats and hats. Sunday was the Lord's day.

Clifford steered Edie to sit by the window. The bus dipped down over the bridge and began to climb towards the long blue backbone of the Peak. Edie leaned forward and watched it coming nearer. Last night Nonny Rees had been in their kitchen, poring over maps spread out on the table as he and Clifford planned this walk together. Nonny was only eighteen, but he seemed almost as much a leader as her father.

Names rolled through Edie's mind: Snake Path, Featherbed Moss, Shining Clough. She heard her father and Nonny saying them every week. Edie loved the sound of those names. They were like spoken jewels. But to her father, they were more than that. She knew that speaking them, he could feel the land under his feet, stones, bog, grass. He could see the contour of the hills as though he was already there. She looked out of the bus window. Her father could have put a name to every clough and crag. But she did not even know where they were going today. She had not asked.

It was the last time she sat like that beside her father, like a stick floating down a river that lets the strong current carry it along without asking where.

Chapter 4

Just for a moment, when she felt the bus stopping, and saw everyone getting up and reaching for rucksacks and jackets, she wasn't sure. There was always this moment, when suddenly the hills came close to the edge of the road and she saw how high and steep they were, and wondered if she could manage. It was her greatest fear that, having won what she most wanted, to walk the hills with her father, she would fail him. That one day she would have to stop halfway, with a pain in her side and her lungs gasping, unable to go on. Of course, her father would stay with her. When she had rested, they would drop down slowly to the road and wait for the others and the bus home. But next Saturday she would be left behind. For the rest of her schooldays, rain or shine, she would have to spend Saturday afternoons shopping. She swore that she would force herself up those slopes, come what might. She wanted to. And anyway, they weren't allowed to climb the highest peaks.

But there was always this moment at the foot of the high hills when she wondered if she could make it. When she wanted the bus to roll on along the road for ever, so that she could enjoy her father's nearness, and the bandied jokes and the songs of the ramblers behind her, and not have to move her legs. Her father had been right not to let Bobby come.

'Hullo.'

She turned with a sudden realisation that someone was speaking to her. A boy she didn't recognise at first was standing beside the path. He spoke quietly and smiled at her shyly from behind spectacles.

'Hullo,' she said doubtfully. 'Are you with us?'

'I hope so. If not, I'm lost already. This is Oldway Youth Club, isn't it?'

Then she knew where she had seen him before.

'Of course! You're Denis Crabtree, aren't you?'

It was the new boy who had come to Sunday School last week. She remembered studying him with curiosity. He had looked different from the other boys — fat Jimmy Greenwood, for instance. There had been a rush of jealousy as she watched him troop off with the senior boys to the Reverend Sutcliffe's Bible class. Edie would have given anything to be in the minister's class, for John Sutcliffe was young and lively with a warm sense of humour. Edie was only eleven, and still in Miss Lancaster's junior class with Mary Bassett. But even when she went up to the seniors, she still wouldn't have John Sutcliffe as her teacher because she was a girl. It wasn't fair.

But today she felt a wave of friendship towards Denis Crabtree, even though he was bigger than herself and a boy. He was still young enough to count as a child, and there were no other children on the ramble. Clifford's youth club from Oldway Chapel were all young men and women; most of them had left school. Walking beside them, feeling them so strong and cheerful and confident all around her, Edith always sensed the weight of responsibility. She musn't hold them up by being too slow, she mustn't let them see that she was tired, she mustn't make anyone worry that she was wet or cold. Seeing someone almost her own age, she felt her burden shared. She found herself smiling back.

'That's Clifford Ramsden over there, isn't it? Is he your father?'

The way he said the name made her feel proud. Everyone seemed to know Clifford Ramsden. They didn't always agree with him about the union and the local elections. But they all respected him. At the mill, where he worked as a tackler. At the chapel, where he led the youth club. Even on the hills, many of the rambling clubs greeted him when they met. He was her father. He had always been special to her. But she was beginning to realise that other people thought he was special too. And she was Clifford Ramsden's daughter. She felt a warm glow of pleasure towards the boy.

'Yes. But you haven't joined the youth club, have you? You're not old enough.'

'I've come with my parents. We only moved to Oldway last week. The Reverend Sutcliffe came round to our house. He said your father needed some help with the club. They're over there.'

Clifford had spread out the map on a boulder. Usually it would have been Nonny leaning over it eagerly, discussing the route. Today he stood in the background, a stocky, brown-haired boy, saying little. He looked almost as if he were sulking. A tall, thin man with glasses was peering at the map as Clifford pointed things out to him.

'Is that your father?'

'Yes. And my mother.'

'Your *mother*!'

A dark-haired woman was holding a box camera in front of her chest, looking down into the viewfinder. She was photographing a group of laughing boys and girls, with their arms linked together. She wore a gaberdine skirt and a man's checked shirt and had yellow woollen socks rolled down round her ankles. Edith's thoughts flew to her own straight-backed mother in the second-best coat and felt hat she wore for Saturday shopping. She strove to picture her here, in yellow woolly socks. The thought was too much for her, and she burst into giggles.

'Did I make a joke?'

'No,' she gasped. 'They're just so different. Come on, look. I think we're starting.'

Nonny Rees was impatient to be off. He was hoisting his rucksack on to his back, beginning to move along the path. The old smile was beginning to light his cross face as he lifted it to the sun and the hills.

'Let's be having you!' he called back to the others. 'We're wasting a good afternoon. This is meant to be a ramble, not a Hollywood screen test.'

Denis's mother laughed and put her camera away. They began to move off down the road. Any other Saturday Edie would have hurried across the grass to fall in behind her father on the cart-track, letting him draw her along in the wake of his great strides. Now she found herself walking easily and companionably beside Denis, matching her steps to his.

'What are you doing, coming to Oldway, anyway? There's no work. Half the town's on the dole, with the mills closing.'

'My father's a reporter. He used to work in Leeds, on the *Yorkshire Post.*' Then the note of pride in his voice died. 'But . . . well, he's joined your *Exchange and Echo*. My mother used to teach history, before she had me.'

They sounded exotic to Edie. Even she had heard of the *Yorkshire Post.* She had never met people like that before. The poshest friend she had was Freda, whose father owned a greengrocer's shop and had hired the Masonic Hall for Freda's birthday party. But even he didn't *write* for a living, except the figures in his accounts.

Edie hadn't noticed the moment when Denis's voice had dropped.

'"Will you walk a little faster?" said the whiting to the snail,

"There's a porpoise close behind us, and he's treading on my tail."'

Edie looked round, startled. Denis's mother was bringing up the rear with two of the youth club boys.

'Don't look so worried, Edie!' Mrs Crabtree laughed. 'I was only joking. You're doing fine.'

She seemed already as much at home as if Edie was the stranger and not the Crabtrees. She even knew everyone's name.

They came round the shoulder of the hill and a valley opened below them. Denis studied the skyline beyond.

'Which one are we going to climb? That's Bleaklow in the distance, isn't it?'

'Is it?' answered Edie. 'I don't know what any of them are called.'

He stopped suddenly on the path, and turned to stare at her. His eyebrows rose above his glasses, giving him an expression of superiority and surprise.

'You don't! I thought you'd have known all of them, being Clifford Ramsden's daughter. Mr Sutcliffe told us that your father's one of the best-known ramblers in Derbyshire, and that he's walked just about every footpath in the Peaks, summer and winter. He said your father knows every fold of these hills like a mother knows her baby's bottom. He once walked from Manchester to Sheffield in a single day, didn't he?'

She couldn't tell him she hadn't known that. She was caught in a crossfire of emotions, part pride that he seemed to think so highly of her father, even though he was only a millworker, and part anger because he had somehow shamed her, expecting something from her that she couldn't give. Every Friday evening she had sat by the kitchen fire, hugging her knees, hearing those magic names that her father and Nonny let fall as they studied the maps. But she hadn't looked at the maps herself. She hadn't shared his plans. She hadn't taken decisions. She had just let him lead her, and not bothered where.

'Well, we won't be climbing Bleaklow today, or any other hill,' she told him crossly.

'Why not?'

It was her turn to stare at him.

'What did they teach you in Leeds? You don't know much, do you? We always stay on the footpaths, round the bottom of the hills. You have to have a permit to climb the mountains. And they don't give permits to people like us.'

Chapter 5

Denis looked at her disbelievingly.

'You mean there's no public footpath to the top? Not on any of these hills?'

'No.'

'But that's daft!'

'Of course it is. It's true, though.'

The path began to climb up the side of the valley. As Edie struggled on, her cheeks grew hot and her legs began to ache. Yet she knew that she was going up the slope more easily than she had ever done before. It was having Denis just in front of her that made the difference. His legs were only a little longer than her own, and if she kept her eyes on his brown socks and boots, she could put her feet where he put his. She did not have to drive herself to keep up with her father's free-ranging stride, or the wild bursts of energy that sent older boys like Nonny bounding ahead without ever stopping to rest.

Besides, Denis kept up a stream of conversation over his shoulder about the move from his grammar school in Leeds to the one in Oldway, and this slowed him down on the stony footpath. Her father had long since disappeared round the shoulder of the hill, and the gap between the two children and the rest of the youth club was steadily lengthening. It was comforting to look back and see Denis's mother and two of the bigger boys still bringing up the rear, deep in conversation.

As they rounded the bend, another valley opened

before them. Sunlight flashed suddenly on water. A wide, clear brook came tumbling down under rowan branches and over mossy stones. Where it levelled out, the path crossed it in a line of stepping-stones. Beyond, the land changed dramatically. The rounded hills rose suddenly into a jumble of scarps and crags.

At the edge of the brook, the others had halted. They were gathered in a close group around Nonny, who seemed to have stopped on the first stepping-stone.

'Come on,' said Denis. 'They must be waiting for us.'

They started to run. Edie knew that they did not need to. Mrs Crabtree was still behind them. But when Denis began to sprint, she ran with him. Magically, she found that the tiredness had gone from her legs. There was a new-found strength in her muscles, pushing her on. She went flying over the black peat path, jumping the puddles of this week's rain.

Denis finished well in front. But Edie didn't mind. She came in flushed and laughing, seeing herself through her father's eyes as she raced towards him, eyes shining, hair loose in the wind. She ran up to him, expecting him to laugh back at her, perhaps to open his arms and catch her and swing her round as he used to when she was a little girl.

But her father was not smiling. He hardly looked at Edie. His ginger head rose above the faces of the youth club as they gathered round the stepping-stones, muttering angrily. Panting and half-scared, Edie squeezed round them till she could see what they were looking at.

A notice had been planted in midstream, facing them. The wooden post was newly cut and the board above it was freshly painted. It read:

PRIVATE PROPERTY

KEEP OUT

By order

To reinforce the message, a double strand of barbed wire, secured to a rowan tree, slanted across the brook, barring the way over the stepping-stones where the water ran deepest. From a post on the other side of the brook it climbed the steep hillside. Already there were tufts of white sheep wool caught on its barbs.

There was fury in Nonny's face.

'What do they mean, "*Private Property*!"' he shouted. 'It's a public footpath, this. You look at the map!'

'Nay, lad, you don't need to tell me,' Edie's father said. 'If I've walked this path once, I've walked it a hundred times, when you lot were still playing *In and Out the Windows* round your mothers' knees. Of course it's a public right of way.' But his own eyes were snapping with anger.

Mrs Crabtree had caught up with them. She looked round at the grim faces.

'What's up?' she asked.

The group parted and Denis showed her the notice.

'Can they do that? Who's put it there?'

'Lord Big-Bug!' exclaimed Nonny bitterly. 'Him as thinks he owns all this. We're too common to walk over his land, frightening the grouse! Now they're even going to turn us off the public footpaths. Well, we'll soon see about that!'

In a few quick bounds he was halfway across the stepping-stones, close to the notice.

'No, wait, Nonny! Above you!'

At Clifford's warning cry, Nonny checked. He balanced swaying on a boulder just in front of the barbed wire, and squinted up into the sun. Like everyone else, Edie followed his stare.

High above the valley, two men stood watching the group. One of them held something crooked over his arm. A black gun dog crouched in the heather at his feet.

'That's them!' shouted Nonny. 'The swine that did it!'

'Yes,' said Clifford. 'They mean business, all right. One of them's got a gun.'

Edie felt a cold shock at the word as though her feet had suddenly plunged in the beck.

'No, surely!' protested Denis's mother. 'They wouldn't use a gun on us!'

'Nay! It hasn't come to shooting folk yet!' A brief smile crinkled Clifford's face, then left it angry again. 'But that shows they're gamekeepers. They put that notice there. Now they're watching to see what we're going to do.'

'I know what I'm going to do!' The water swirled past Nonny's feet. 'That wire wouldn't keep a rheumatic rabbit out. Your Edie could be under it in two shakes of a terrier's tail. And so can the rest of us. By! I wish I'd brought a pair of wire-cutters. I'd be through that quicker than you can break a flea's knees. And I'll show them what they can do with their notice!'

At his shout the black labrador leaped to its feet. The gamekeeper motioned it down. But now the two men were coming closer to the brook, with the dog creeping behind them through the heather. Edie could see them clearly — the hats, the tweed suits, the long barrel of the shotgun folded over one arm.

Her scared gaze went to her father's face. She saw his eyes meet Mr Crabtree's. The two men shook their heads.

'Nay, lad. Leave it. I'm responsible for this lot. It's not the right time to make trouble.'

Nonny's scowl darkened. Before the Crabtrees came, he and Clifford had always been the ones who made the decisions.

'It's the right place, though, isn't it?' Nonny stood defiantly in midstream with the water sweeping round him. 'Are you going to turn round and let him get away with this? Does he think just because he's a duke and I sweep a mill floor that gives him the right to own everything? This path belongs to us, any road!'

'Oh, it's ours, all right.' Edie watched her father fighting to keep down his own anger as he turned back from the brook. 'That path has always belonged to folk.' He lifted his eyes to the skyline and added softly. 'And so do the hills, by my reckoning. It's the same hand made us and them.'

Denis's father was making notes in a little black book. Edie's father strode past him.

'If that's for your newspaper, you're wasting your time. It's happening every week. First they tell us we haven't to move off the footpaths, and then they close them. Folks don't want to read what they know already.'

Mr Crabtree laughed. 'I see what you mean. It's not going to double the circulation of the *Exchange and Echo*, is it?'

That was too much for Nonny. He came leaping back on to the bank and stood in front of the reporter.

'If it's headlines you want, you'll get them before long! I've had just about enough. Never mind the footpath. I want to climb these hills and walk on the tops. Just let them try and stop me, with their guns and their dogs, and see what happens then! *That'll* make a story for you, if it's blood you're looking for.'

'Steady, lad. We're not looking for a fight.' Clifford laid a hand on his shoulder. 'Losing your temper won't help.'

'Won't it? Happen it's the only thing that will!'

'You'll damage yourself and you'll not shift them.'

The young man and the older one stared at each other, each battling with his anger.

'Where to now?' asked Mrs Crabtree, trying to ease the situation.

'Back the way we came. Where else? We've no choice.'

There was a groan of disappointment from the youth club. This was what they hated most. To trudge the wearying climb up from the road, and then, just when the highest hills came into sight, to have to turn back down the same path. Never to scale the real peaks. Never to stand with the mountain wind blowing round them and see four counties rolling away beneath them. Always to be shepherded on to the crowded footpaths, winding along the valleys and the humbler slopes.

Only Edie felt a wave of relief. The wire, the forbidding notice, the gun, had frightened her. The brook had turned cold and the countryside unfriendly. She shivered. She had walked a long way already. She would be glad to turn back, though nothing would have made her admit it.

She glanced sideways at Denis, wondering if he shared her feelings. But to her surprise his gaze was still fixed on Nonny. His eyes sparkled behind his glasses. He was smiling to himself, as though in excitement.

Nonny stood mutinously still as the others started back down the path they had come by. Edie fell in close beside her father. As they rounded the bend that hid the brook, Denis kept looking back.

'Where's Nonny?' asked Clifford. 'Daft beggar.'

Two angry shouts rang out behind them. A dog barked furiously. Nonny came running round the bend in the path, his legs dripping water. He was dragging the white-painted notice-board with him.

He looked over his shoulder, laughing excitedly. Then he hurled the board to the ground.

'Nay, lad. You shouldn't have done that,' warned Clifford. 'They'll be on to you now.'

'Pigs!' cried Nonny. 'We're as good as they are! Who are they to tell us where we can put our boots and where we can't? Well, I'll show their boss where I'm going to put mine. Right through his notice!'

He jumped on it with his strong, nailed boots. There was a savage crack which echoed round the hills as the painted words broke into splinters.

Edie gasped. But Denis darted forward and danced up and down on the pieces too.

'Take *that*! And *that*!' he laughed.

Out of sight, the valley rang with the dog's barking.

Chapter 6

Nonny pushed his way to his usual place at the front of the line. Edie felt a pang of disappointment as Denis hurried after him.

Clifford lengthened his stride, swinging Edie's hand between them. He sang out to the others, with a pretence of cheerfulness, 'Come on, then! Let's be having you.

'*John Brown's body lies a-mouldering in the grave . . .*'

They shouted back the chorus.

'*But his soul goes marching on.*'

Nonny called over his shoulder bitterly, 'Aye, and they say there are some keepers will even stop you singing on the footpaths now, in case you frighten the grouse!'

At that, everyone raised their voices louder. Edie felt better as she sang with them. This was more like it used to be. There had been a few moments back there at the stepping-stones, with the threatening keepers and the dog, when she had almost wished herself safe beside her mother and Bobby, looking in the window of the Co-op at clothes and furniture they weren't going to buy.

As they rounded the next turn, they came face to face with a party of ramblers coming the other way. The Oldway club stepped off on to the grass to make way for them, and Nonny called out, 'You're wasting your time. His Lordship's wired off the stepping-stones at Yellow-slacks. You'll not get through without the keepers spotting you.'

'Get away,' laughed their leader. 'They never have. It's a designated footpath, this.'

'You'll see,' said Clifford. 'Though you'll happen have a job finding his notice!'

There was a murmur of protest along the line of newcomers, then the party went on towards the brook.

Edie found herself beside Denis again as they waited for them to pass.

'Can they really stop people singing?' he asked. 'It's not against the law.'

'They can do what they like. They own all this. They don't really want us here at all. By rights, we're breaking the law just standing on the grass like this.'

Far down the valley there were flashes of colour. White, red, yellow, green. The knitted caps and pullovers of other ramblers. Edie counted three, four, five more groups toiling up the same path.

'It's like blooming Piccadilly,' grumbled Nonny, stepping back on to the trampled mud. 'One path. And now that doesn't go anywhere.'

Laughter crinkled the corners of Mrs Crabtree's eyes.

'I think we should leave a bit more room for the others. Those gamekeepers are out of sight now. What do you say, Nonny? Why don't we take a quick climb up the next hill to cheer ourselves up? There's plenty of time before the bus.'

'Get away. There's no footpath up Wash Brow. Just the one we're on, and they've closed that off now.'

'We don't need a footpath, do we? It's a clear day. When we get to the top we'll be able to see our way back to the road. We can't get lost.'

'Who's talking about getting lost? By! You Crabtrees are green. A footpath's a footpath. And that's all we're allowed; not a yard on either side of it.'

Edie's father sighed. 'Nonny's right. The keepers know my face, and if Nonny's smashed their notice, we'll be in their bad books already. If they were to black this club, they could get us turned off every path in the Peaks.'

'They wouldn't do that, would they?'

'I wouldn't try them.'

'All the same, they're a long way back. And what the eye don't see . . .'

Edie looked at the expectant faces all around her, at Nonny's scowl. A smile of mischief was lighting Denis's face like his mother's. She saw her father raise his eyebrows at Mr Crabtree. Denis's father shrugged his shoulders and grinned.

'I'm game, if you are.'

Suddenly Edie's own father's eyes began to twinkle like a young boy's.

'You're on, then! But don't say I didn't warn you.'

With a cry of joy, the boys and girls began to scramble up the hillside, with Nonny in the lead. The squelching puddles of the track gave way to dry, crumbling peat and the rustle of last year's heather. As they climbed out of the valley they could hear the wind in their ears.

Edie struggled after them. It was not a very big hill, but she felt her breath rasping painfully in her chest and a pulse thumping in her head. She kept looking at the skyline, fixing her eyes on a rock or a clump of heather that must mark the summit. But every time she hauled herself up to it, she saw the slope of the hill stretching endlessly on beyond. After a while she stopped looking up and fixed her eyes on the ground just in front of her hands.

She had her head down, telling herself that she couldn't keep going any longer, that she must stop and rest, when she almost fell over Denis's boots. He had halted just in front of her. She was pleased to see that he was gasping for breath as well.

But the rest of the party had stopped too. This time, the

murmuring was angrier. Edie pulled herself up the last few yards to stand beside her father. He grasped her hand almost absentmindedly.

'Are you all right, chuck?'

He was looking at something else. Nonny had climbed on to a boulder. The wind was tugging at his brown hair.

They were all staring down over the side of the ridge into the valley they had left behind. Edie could see the white of the waterfalls. The two gamekeepers were running down the far slope towards the brook. One of them cupped his hands to his mouth. His voice floated up to them.

'What do you think you're doing up there? You're on private property. Come down at once, or I'll set the dog on you.'

The other party of ramblers had halted in front of the stepping-stones. Their upturned faces watched.

'Now will you believe me?' Nonny shouted at Mrs Crabtree. 'We've as much freedom to roam as a clockwork train. They think they can wind us up at Saturday dinner-time and put us on a single track, and by tea-time we'll have run out of steam. They can put us away in a box and keep us there for the rest of the week, while they have all this for themselves.'

'They'd never catch us,' grinned Denis. 'We could be down the other side of the hill and back to the road before the dog got anywhere near us.'

But this time Edie's father shook his head. 'Best not. We're in trouble enough already.'

Mrs Crabtree tried to cheer them up. 'They can't really prosecute us for trespass, you know. All we have to do is to offer them sixpence to pay for any damage we've caused, and there's nothing they can do.'

Clifford Ramsden stared at her bitterly. 'You don't know what this is all about, do you? It's not just money. We're not one of your posh rambling clubs. "Terribly sorry, my good man. There's sixpence for you." We're working folk, us. Five and a half days a week, slaving in a cotton mill for them. Our lungs clogged full of fluff, so their pockets can be full of money. And you say it's us should be paying *them* for damage?'

'Get down, I said!' a voice yelled from the valley.

'Come on,' said Mr Crabtree quietly. 'I think it's back to the path.'

Edie looked regretfully at the last rolling slope above her. She had got her breath back, and her legs had stopped aching. She could have reached the summit this time; she knew she could. All that effort for nothing. The others were trooping sullenly past her, back down the slope up which they had just toiled.

Only Nonny stood his ground obstinately. He was staring away from the valley, across the mountains to the south.

'I'll not be forbidden,' he muttered. 'I'm going to climb the biggest one of all. Kinder Scout. And I dare them to stop me.'

Then he leaped off the boulder and began to run downhill after the others.

'Can I borrow the map?' called Denis, as he went past them.

'You won't need a scholarship to find the road,' said Nonny, tossing it so that it fell just out of Denis's reach. 'They've only left us one way.'

But Denis retrieved the map and spread it out in the heather. His finger strayed over the contour lines and the marks of the crags. Then it came to rest, and he lifted his eyes southwards to the jumbled peaks and valleys.

'That's it!' he said softly. 'Kinder Scout. Nonny's right. Look! The highest of the lot, and not a single footpath crossing it.'

'Where?' asked Edith, shading her eyes as she stared at the confusion of moorland.

'There! Right above the lot.'

Once her eyes had found it, there was no mistaking Kinder Scout. Above all the misty crags and cloughs, a single massive ridge marched right across the skyline. There was no graceful peak, no gentle slopes. The fast-declining sun of the March afternoon threw the sheer northern face into forbidding shadow. Before its bulk, Edith felt awed and small.

'Nonny's going to climb that,' said Denis. 'And I'll tell you something else. When he does, I'm going with him.'

Again she felt that stab of envy. Then a daring new thought, like the first spear of a plant thrusting up under the soil, began to prickle in Edith's mind. But she looked at the dark immensity of Kinder Scout, and she could not find the courage to put her thought into words.

She told him instead, 'My dad says, if you really want a thing enough, you'll find a way to make it happen.'

But she knew she was really speaking to herself.

Chapter 7

Riding home on the bus, back towards the town, Edie knew that today had been different. Other Saturdays she would have snuggled against her father's arm, tired and sleepy, her skin burning where the Pennine wind had scoured it, and her legs limp, like a rag doll filled with sawdust. But not today.

She sat up and looked round the bus. She had half hoped that Denis Crabtree would sit beside her. But he had pushed past, following Nonny to the back of the bus. It hadn't worked, though. The back seat was always reserved for the oldest boys and girls. He had been left red-faced to take the empty seat beside Annie Burton.

From the expressions on all their faces, everyone else had had a bad day. But she felt proud of herself. Oddly enough, she didn't feel as tired as usual, even though she had done a steeper climb than other days. Perhaps it was having Denis to walk with, matching her legs against his instead of trying to fit her steps behind her father's long strides. Perhaps it was having someone her own age to talk to about school and rambling and parents, instead of walking with her father and Nonny, listening to arguments and jokes she only half understood. Or perhaps the hiking itself was making her stronger.

Whatever it was, she found herself suddenly wanting to ask questions.

Nonny was still angry.

'What right has he got to close a public footpath? Who's he to tell us where we can walk and where we can't? Just because he's a duke! I bet you he inherited his title from some robber baron hundreds of years ago, or a king's bastard born the wrong side of the blanket. Does that make him any better than we are?'

'We'll have less of that language,' Clifford told him sharply.

'But why?' Edie asked. 'Why wouldn't they let us cross the brook? Why won't they let us climb the hills?'

'It's the grouse, lass,' her father explained. 'The red grouse. Some little bird that's happened to pick Kinder Scout and the moors hereabouts for its home. They'll be nesting soon. And the Duke and the other landowners don't want folk like us disturbing the chicks. Because, come August, they'll be out there with their guns, him and Her Grace and all their fine friends, banging away and killing everything that moves.'

'But they can't blame us! *We* wouldn't kill them.'

There was a roar of laughter from the back seat. Nonny called out, 'Nay, you've got a lot to learn, Edie! You've put yourself in the wrong class, by saying that. To be one of them, you have to *like* killing. Anything in sight. Deer, grouse, ducks, fish. You name it, they'll kill it, stone dead. It's their idea of fun, you see. They're brought up to it.'

'Well, look at it this way. It's cheaper than war,' said Denis's father reasonably. 'Easier on the peasants, too. It's better to be paid as a beater than be carted off to some foreign country to have your head blown off or your guts carved out, isn't it?'

'Who are you calling a peasant?' growled Nonny.

'But they're not shooting now,' Edie said.

'No,' retorted Nonny. 'But Lady Muck doesn't want to eat a bird that's been fed off the same ground Edie Ramsden's trodden on. Look at your feet. Common as sneezing, you are.'

Edie wriggled her toes inside her muddy boots.

'I don't care,' she said proudly.

'Good for you, Edie,' Mrs Crabtree told her. 'You hold your head up. Don't let them make you ashamed of what you are. I've yet to meet a duke that was the equal of your father.'

'Meet a lot of dukes, do you?' asked Clifford, winking at Edie. 'I don't know as you Crabtrees are fit company for millworkers. Do you have them round for supper every Saturday night?'

'Get away with you,' Mrs Crabtree laughed. 'Edie knows what I mean.'

In the back seat, the girls began to sing *The Road to the Isles*.

The twilight descended suddenly round them. It was not just the setting sun, slipping down into the distant Mersey. The smoke from a hundred thousand chimneys closed around them. They were back in the town.

Chapter 8

Edie had escaped from Saturday afternoon shopping, but not from Saturday evening. She could not avoid hair-washing and bath night. Her mother poured buckets of hot water into the zinc bath, laying towels on the hearthrug in front of the fire. Bobby went first, and then Edie. The peat from Wash Brow and the ash of the burnt heather clouded the water, washing away the countryside for another week. By the time it was her father's turn to use the water, it would be almost the colour of oxtail soup.

While her father bathed, her mother took Edie into the scullery to wash her hair. Edie hung over the sink, while hard fingers worked the lather into her scalp, and the stinging suds trickled into the corners of her eyes. The best bit was afterwards, when she had mopped the worst of the wet and taken a warm, dry towel from the airing cupboard. Back in the kitchen her father, dressed again, and looking strangely pink and scrubbed ready for Sunday, put down the pack of cards on which he had been counting cribbage scores, and opened his knees wide so that she could sit on the hearthrug between them. He towelled her hair dry with huge, strong hands that were strangely gentle. Edie sat, cosy in her dressing-gown, rocked by those hands, her half-closed eyes finding pictures in the glowing coals.

'Bedtime,' said Maggie to Bobby.

'Do I have to?'

'Yes. You, too, in half an hour, Edie.'

'It's not fair. Won't I ever go to bed after her?'

'I dare say. When she's an old lady of sixty, and you're a young fellow of fifty-seven.'

Bobby went upstairs grumbling.

There was a rap at the door. Her father pushed Edie gently off his knees.

'Off to your mother. That'll be Nonny.' He called out, 'Come in. The door's on the latch.'

Reluctantly, Edie moved across to the other side of the fireplace as the door flew open. Nonny burst in, laughing and unwinding a muffler from his neck with a flourish, and smelling of fish and chips. All the bad temper of the afternoon had gone. He seemed to fill the room with his energy.

'Hullo, Topsy,' he teased, rumpling her damp tangles.

Edie blushed and smiled. She never knew how to speak to Nonny. He was too young to be an adopted uncle. Not a bit like her real Uncle Ted, who had a moustache and said, 'My, lass, you've grown another inch!' every time he saw her.

Nonny was only eighteen, but he and Edie's father were firm friends. They worked at the same mill. Nonny was always round at the house, talking youth club business, politics, rambling. They were often arguing, their eyes bright as clashing swords, about what could and could not be done. Edie could not understand a quarter of what they said, but it always ended in laughter, Clifford clapping Nonny on the shoulder and sealing their friendship with a cup of cocoa round the fire. Long ago, Maggie Ramsden had taught Nonny in Sunday School. She still liked him, though she never let it sound as though she did.

This time Edie strained to hear what they were saying. As they talked, Maggie tugged the comb through Edie's hair. Then came the curlers: strips of old pillowcase twisted round each lock of hair, rolled up and tied tightly at the top.

And always there were little wisps of hair caught out of place in the knot and pulling painfully at the roots. No amount of pillows could soften the hard lumps of those curlers. On Saturday nights it was like trying to sleep with her head in a coal-scuttle. All for one day in the week.

She twisted her head away from her mother's hands to listen.

'What are you looking so cheerful about, all of a sudden?'

'I met this lot down the chip shop. I told them what happened today. And they say they go out every Sunday with maps, wire-cutters, the whole works. If they find the beggars have wired up the path, they just cut through it, like a red-hot poker through butter, and carry on. They're not going to stop till they've cleared every footpath in the Peaks.'

'They'll be asking for trouble, then,' Maggie said. 'Doing damage to private property.'

Nonny swung round eagerly. 'That's just the point, Maggie! It's not their property. It's a public footpath. They'd no right to put that wire up in the first place. That's what we should have done today at Yellowslacks.'

'With two keepers watching? A shotgun, and a dog? What did you say this bunch of rebels were called?'

'The North Derbyshire Young Workers Recreation Club. But Lil — that's the girl that organises them — she says they call themselves Red Grouse for short.'

'I'm not surprised, with a title like that. You'd have a job saying that with a mouthful of chip butty!'

Maggie Ramsden spoke sharply. 'It sounds as though there'll be a few Communists amongst that lot, with a name like that.'

Edie winced as another curler knotted tightly. She didn't know what Communists were, but the way her mother said the word made them sound dangerous.

'What if there are? So long as they're on our side.'

Edie's father looked thoughtful. 'They've some daft ideas, to my way of thinking. But I've met good and bad among them, like the rest of us.'

Nonny cocked his head on one side. His eyes twinkled mischievously.

'Well? How about it, Clifford? They're going down Shelf Brook tomorrow. Lil says there's a rumour they've closed Doctor's Gate as well. Red Grouse have sworn they're going to open up the length of it, from the Old Woman to Yellowslacks. Just think of it. A whole day on the moors. All the way down the Shelf Brook. Look!'

He threw a map down on the kitchen table and pointed.

Edie started forward. Not tomorrow. She and her father couldn't go rambling tomorrow. Her mother said what Edie was thinking.

'Tomorrow's Sunday.'

Nonny's eyes still coaxed Clifford. 'Well, you know what they say. The better the day, the better the deed.'

Clifford shook his head. 'We're chapel folk, Nonny. Twice every Sunday. I've never missed, and nor have you.'

'I'll tell the Reverend Sutcliffe. There's a reason this time. He'll know I'm doing right.'

'He won't!' said Maggie.

Edie looked from one to the other in alarm. She knew that every Sunday morning the streets were packed with people streaming towards the buses and the trains, pouring out into the countryside from the smoky towns. But not the Ramsden family, not Nonny Rees. Their rambling was only done on Saturdays. On Sundays they walked against the tide, up the hill to Oldway Chapel in their best clothes. Miss Lancaster said if you didn't go to chapel you went to hell.

Her father must have seen her face. 'Time you were in bed, chuck. Help me get the supper.'

She mixed the cocoa, while he cut the bread and cheese. Then she kissed her mother and father goodnight.

'What about me?' Nonny said, his eyes dancing. 'Don't I get one?'

Edie blushed and dodged away. 'Goodnight!' she gasped, and bolted from the room before he could catch her.

She tiptoed into the bedroom where Bobby was already asleep. His dressing-gown had fallen on the floor. She laid her knobbly head uncomfortably on her pillow and shut her eyes. Tomorrow was Sunday. Bacon and eggs for breakfast. Her father's strong voice singing beside her in chapel. He would be home with them all day.

But sleep would not come. As she tossed her head, she was remembering a jumble of moorland, stained with dying light like blackberry juice, a map spread out in the heather. Kinder Scout.

Chapter 9

Edie made a face in the mirror as she unknotted the strips of cloth in which her hair was rolled. She could see her brother Bobby peeping at her from under the bedclothes.

She hated those Sunday curls. All week her brown hair hung limp and straight. Now tight corkscrews stuck out all round her head. She brushed at them furiously. She had not been able to sleep properly with her head on those hard lumps. It wasn't worth the agony. Before the end of the day these curls would be drooping over her shoulders like sagging bed-springs. By Monday morning they would have disappeared.

She liked her Saturday self, in jumper and skirt, her straight hair tied back with a ribbon. It was the self that belonged to her father, when they escaped from the town and went off to the hills together.

But on Sunday she could have him all day. She pulled on her best dress, emerald green wool, with a tartan collar. It was only the fourth time she had worn it, and it hadn't been washed. The new wool was scratchy on her arms.

Her mother had made that dress specially for Freda's birthday party. Edie had put it on proudly. But when she came home, she didn't say that every other girl in the Masonic Hall had worn a party frock of taffeta or velvet. Edith had been the only one in a home-made woollen dress.

She came downstairs in her best dress and her slippers. The tiles of the passage shone cleanly and there were fresh flowers on the hall table. Her mother always finished the Saturday shopping by buying a bunch of flowers from the market for Sunday. There was a smell of bacon and eggs from the kitchen.

She opened the door slowly. This was one of the best moments. For six days of the week, she did not see her father in the morning. He had breakfasted and was off to the mill before her mother woke her. The most she might get was his voice calling goodbye up the stairs. But Sundays were special. He would be sitting in the armchair, reading the Sunday paper. They would have breakfast together. Then he would polish the family's shoes and they would walk to chapel together.

'Hullo, love,' he said, looking up.

But his smile didn't seem to reach out and embrace her as it usually did. There was something wrong. The plate in front of him was already empty.

'You're looking very smart.' Why did he sound as if he was trying to coax her? 'Is that a new dress?'

'No, silly. I had it for Freda's party. You remember.'

And then she realised. Her father wasn't wearing his own Sunday clothes. He should have had on a clean white shirt with a starched collar and the trousers of his dark grey chapel suit, even if he did pull on an old green cardigan till after breakfast. But he was sitting opposite her in his corduroy trousers and his big woollen socks and the flannel shirt he had worn yesterday. As if this was Saturday, and he was off for an afternoon's ramble with the youth club.

She glanced at her mother in a sudden fear that she had got the wrong day. It had been Saturday yesterday, hadn't it? Her mother never put on her best dress till half an hour before they went to chapel. But it must be Sunday. She was frying bacon and eggs. All through the week, it was bacon one day, eggs the next, scrambled, poached or boiled. But you only got bacon *and* eggs for Sunday breakfast.

Maggie's back was even stiffer than usual. The metal slice

rattled against the side of the pan. 'You'll miss that bus,' she said to her husband, sharply.

She pushed his snap tin filled with sandwiches across the table, her normally brisk movements made jerky with anger.

'You'll be needing that, I suppose.'

'Thanks, love. You're a good lass. I knew you'd understand.'

'I *don't* understand. Thirteen years we've been married. And it's the first time you've missed going to chapel. That Nonny Rees!'

Edie stared from one parent to another. The back door rattled. Before anyone could answer it, Nonny burst into the kitchen. His brown eyes were dancing with mischief. He was dressed like Clifford in old trousers, pullover, walking boots, with a rucksack on his back. The browns and greens and yellows of their hiking clothes would be almost lost on the grassy hills, but here in the Sunday grey of the millworkers' cottages the colours shouted like tropical parrots.

'Morning, Curlilocks. That's a smart frock. Best watch the leprechauns don't get you, wearing the green like that.'

His hand rumpled Edie's Sunday curls. Not hard like her mother's, or gentle like her dad's, but teasing.

'Morning, Maggie.'

Edie's mother turned back to the stove and would not look at either of them. Nonny winked at Clifford.

'I saw Mrs Greenwood in her back yard as I came past. She gave me a funny look, and all.'

'Aye, and she'll not be the only one.' Edie's father looked at his own rucksack with indecision. Edie crossed her fingers. He couldn't go without her, he mustn't. But he grasped the webbing strap and swung the rucksack on to his back.

'I'm a Ramsden. There's only One tells me what's right and what's wrong. Are you fit, then?'

He gave Edie a hug. 'Bye, chuck. Be a good girl and help your mam.'

He looked regretfully at his wife's straight back.

'I'll be back for tea-time.'

She did not turn. He dropped a kiss on the back of her neck. There was a brief glimpse of sunshine as the door opened on the yard, and then they were gone. Without the two of them, the house seemed suddenly lifeless. Then Maggie turned. For several minutes she and Edie stared at the closed door in silence.

'Where have they gone?' Edie asked in a small, lost voice, though she knew well enough.

'Rambling, *they* call it. And somewhere they've no business to be going, by the sound of it. Men! They'll go galloping off like knights in shining armour, and leave us to fight their battles nearer home.'

She slammed a plate of breakfast in front of Edie. Edie stared down at it. Resentment burned in her, as great as her mother's, but for a different reason. Behind the kitchen door were her own walking boots, with shiny new cleats hammered into the toes and heels. They had been a Christmas present from her father. Last night she had cleaned the mud from them and rubbed dubbin into the leather. Now they stood waiting for another Saturday. But not for today.

Today was Sunday. On Sunday morning the whole Ramsden family went to chapel together. And in the afternoon it was Sunday School. She couldn't miss it. If you didn't go to chapel you went to hell. Miss Lancaster had said so. Her father knew she couldn't go rambling on Sunday. But he had gone, and left her without him all day.

Bobby stood in the doorway, rubbing the sleep from his eyes.

'Where did Dad go?' he asked.
'Rambling,' said Edie bleakly.
'Trespassing,' snapped his mother.

Chapter 10

'Why are we going so fast?' asked Bobby, dragging along the pavement towards chapel.

'Because you took so long eating your breakfast,' retorted his mother, pulling him after her, though he was really too old to hold her hand.

Edie knew that was not the reason. They were quite early. She felt the tension in her mother and understood it. For the first time in thirteen years Clifford Ramsden's place in chapel would be empty. It was her mother who would have to meet the curious stares and whispers.

Edie hurried beside her mother, matching her brisk steps, as she tried to match her father's strides on the hills. She drew herself up taller, walking shoulder to shoulder with her mother, doing her best to fill the gap her father had left. It was the only way she could show that she was still loyal to him. She could not tell if it helped.

Down in their street, cloud had settled dully over the rooftops as the coal fires were lit. The mill chimney at the end of the road loomed through the murk. But as they climbed the hill to Oldway Chapel they came out into a thinner, bluer air. Edie breathed deeply, and turned for a moment, looking south-east over the roofs of the town.

She caught her breath. She had not realised she could see it even from here. But now that she knew its outline, there was no mistaking it on the distant skyline. Kinder Scout. All these years she had been looking at it without knowing its name.

'We're too late,' muttered her mother.

Already the soberly-dressed congregation was being drawn in through the chapel gateway, like lines of iron filings to a magnet. Mrs Greenwood was there, with fat Jimmy grinning at Edie from behind her back.

'Where's your dad, then?' he called out as the Ramsdens approached.

Edie drew a sharp breath. 'He was called away.'

'On business,' said her mother shortly.

Edie looked up, startled. Did that count as a lie?

Mrs Greenwood's eyes widened. 'Oh? Funny sort of business, if you ask me. I saw him going down our street this morning with a rucksack on his back.'

'You know he runs the youth club. He takes them rambling, if he can find anywhere left for them to go.'

'I should have thought he'd have been in chapel, then, on Sunday morning, setting them a good example.'

'And where's your Bert, then, Mrs Greenwood?'

Jimmy's mother stiffened. 'At home with his bronchitis. You know how he suffers with his chest.'

'He should take up hiking, then! A good tramp over the moors would do his lungs more good than sitting over a fire. And my husband's been needing help with that club these last two years.'

This time, Edie could not resist a victorious grin in Jimmy Greenwood's direction. Margaret Ramsden was as much a fighter as her husband in her own way.

A lean figure bounded in at the side gate. The Reverend Sutcliffe came running towards them, his black gown flying out over one shoulder. He smiled at them all and clasped Maggie warmly by the hand.

'So he went, after all? *And the Lord called Moses to the top of the mountain.*' He burst out laughing. 'Don't look so shocked, Maggie! Nonny's told me what they're up to.

He'll be back with us for this evening's service. I know I can trust him for that.'

He turned to Edie. For one moment she thought he was going to rumple those awful curls too. Instead, he shook her hand, as though she was grown-up.

'You must be proud of your father, Edie. There aren't enough like him. I wish I could join them myself. It's a job that needs doing. But I can hardly take Sunday morning off in my line of business, can I?'

And he swept them with him into the safety of the chapel.

It was the first time Edie had asked herself whether she minded going to church. Until today, it had been as inevitable as sunrise. Chapel for all of them in the morning. Sunday School with Bobby in the afternoon. Chapel again for her parents in the evening while Edie stayed at home and saw Bobby into bed. Until her father started to take her on the Saturday rambles, this had been her favourite day. In chapel, for a whole hour, she could sit next to her father, who had so little time to spend with her during the week. The four of them, close together in one pew. Ramsdens. A warm, strong family. Her dad's special smile to her as the organ struck up one of his favourite hymns. Seeing him stand up tall and vigorous beside her and throw back his head. Hearing his rich bass voice ring out above the choir. They were always wanting him to join the choir, but he wouldn't, because choir practice was Thursday night, and Thursday night was union meeting. There had been more than one argument about that. But her father was adamant that union business was God's business, and he was more needed there than he was in the choir. But every Christmas he sang in the *Messiah*.

So Edie never minded if the sermons were long and difficult to understand. She could lean against the warmth of her father's arm, and he would smile down at her and open the crook of his elbow to settle her closer.

Today she felt suddenly bereaved. There was just her mother beside her in the pew, with Bobby beyond. And a great, cold, empty space on her left, where her father should have been. There was a cold, empty space in her heart too, because he hadn't told her what he was doing, he hadn't asked her to come. He had broken the pattern of a lifetime. He had put on his hiking clothes and gone off with Nonny Rees, the two of them laughing guiltily like naughty schoolboys. And he had left her behind.

She looked up, and her spirits rose suddenly. She had forgotten Denis Crabtree. He was sitting with his parents in a pew on the other side of the church, looking older and smarter in his grammar school blazer. He smiled at her across the aisle as though he was really pleased to see her. Edie flushed with pleasure. When she looked round, Mary Bassett was staring at them both. Edie found herself looking forward to Sunday School more than usual.

Chapter 11

After all, her father was home quite early.

Denis Crabtree had been in Sunday School. The other senior boys would never speak to the junior girls, but he had greeted her in front of all the others like an old friend.

'Will your father be going out again next week?' he had asked.

'Of course! We always go.' She had crossed her fingers, praying that the weather would not turn bad. It was more important than ever now not to be left behind.

Later, in the juniors' room, Mary Bassett had not been able to restrain her curiosity. When Edie had told her all she knew about the Crabtrees, Mary had sniffed.

'I should have thought he was a bit too posh for someone like you.'

'He's not! We're as good as them, any day,' Edie answered fiercely.

But afterwards, no one had met Edie and Bobby. There had been no Sunday afternoon stroll with their parents over the tops, taking the long way home for the sake of the walk.

They only used the front room on Sundays. Edie was curled up in an armchair, reading, keeping her feet out of the way of Bobby, who was laying out his train set on the floor. As the kitchen door banged, Maggie Ramsden looked up from the letter she was writing. The door of the front room opened and Clifford's face looked round. He padded across the carpet in muddy socks.

'Did you miss me?'

He fondled Edie's drooping curls.

'You mind what you're doing with those dirty hands,' said Maggie. 'I only washed her hair last night.'

'You won't want a kiss, then,' he teased his wife.

But he hugged her all the same.

'Go on with you. I've kept you a roast dinner. I've put it on a saucepan of hot water to keep warm.'

Edie felt the anger drain out of her mother. The house was at peace again. She let herself relax happily, like a swing between two strong trees.

After tea, her parents went off to chapel, as if it had been any other Sunday. When Bobby was in bed and the house was quiet, she went back to the kitchen. Her father's boots were there, still caked with black peat around the welts. She carried them out into the yard and scraped off the mud with an old knife. She didn't have to do this. He would have seen to it himself after chapel. But it wasn't a deed of love. She hoped it would make him feel guilty because he had been away all day without her. As the black pellets dropped on to the ground, she stared down at them, wondering what hills they had come from.

Back in the kitchen, she worked dubbin into the scuffed leather and set the boots behind the kitchen door beside her own. Now when he came back, she would forgive him.

'Where have you been? Did you go back to the stepping-stones?' she asked him.

He lifted her on to his knee, making up for that lonely hour in chapel.

'We made for the other end of Doctor's Gate. The beggars had wired that up, too. But it would take more than a few strands of barbed wire to stop that lot. Nonny had his wire-cutters out, and we were over that stile before you could say "Private Property". And then it was such a grand day we climbed up Shelf Moor all the way to the Pike.'

'So you *have* been trespassing?' Maggie said.

'Well, they'd no right to shut off a public footpath in the first place.'

'You've not stayed on the path if you climbed the Pike.'

'Aye, lass!' he chuckled. 'You've caught me out there.'

'Didn't the keepers stop you?' asked Edie, wide-eyed.

'That was the daft thing. We didn't see a keeper all day. I think young Lil was getting quite disappointed. She's a firebrand, that one. But she had the last laugh.

'We'd just come down off the heather on to the road, when this great Rolls Royce comes over the brow of the hill. And who should it be but the Duke himself! Of course, he knew where we'd been. He stops the car and shouts, "What do you mean, trespassing on my land?" And Lil, she bursts out singing *The Red Flag*, and all the rest of them joined in. Laugh? I thought the old Duke was going to burst a blood vessel. But we were back on the road, so there was nothing he could do to us.'

'You'll come to no good, getting mixed up with folk like that,' Maggie scolded.

'Get away. There's no harm in them. They're young and just a bit wild, that's all.'

'You ought to know better at your age. They'll land you in trouble, you mark my words.'

'I'll answer for what I do and I'll choose the company I keep. It was a rare day we had together.'

He stared into the flickering coals, hugging Edie closer.

'I wish you could have been there, our Edie. On the tops of the hills, on a Sunday morning. The sky bigger than you can ever imagine in town. And the quiet. At first it's so still it seems to shout at you. And then you realise it isn't quiet at all. There's the dried heather rustling in the wind, and the sheep calling to each other, and the buzzards crying. And there wasn't a soul in sight, anywhere we looked.'

The smile faded. There was a long silence.

'It's not like the footpaths, with hundreds of folk all shuffling past each other, like going through mill gates on Monday morning. But that's all they've left us now, by law.

'I can't swallow it, that one man can own a mountain and keep the rest of us off. I wouldn't think I *owned* a thing like Bleaklow or Kinder Scout, no matter how many documents the lawyers gave me. A mountain's more than that. No one can own it. It's God's gift. He gave it to all of us, free, to use and look after and pass on when we've gone.'

A coal fell from the fire. He set Edie down.

'It's past your bedtime, chuck.'

'Do I have to go?' she asked like Bobby, clinging still.

The weekend seemed to be over almost before it had begun. Tomorrow was Monday. School for her, the spinning mill for him. It would be a whole week before they could be together again.

Chapter 12

But when she boarded the bus on Saturday, her spirits soared because Denis Crabtree had come a second time. He was smiling at her from behind his glasses. For a moment she thought she might be bold enough to go and sit beside him. But then shyness overtook her, and she slipped into her usual place beside her father. All the same, her heart was beating unexpectedly fast under her Fair Isle jumper. She could feel her cheeks flushing. Perhaps Uncle Ted was right after all. Perhaps you did grow up in leaps and bounds that took people by surprise, including yourself.

She tried to remember where they were going today. Cowgill Force. Nonny had been in the kitchen last night, with the map spread out across the table. This time, she had got up to look.

She came to with a start as the bus stopped well short of the moors and tipped them all out on the grass verge. She found Denis quickly.

'Hullo. How's your new school going?'

'It's not so bad. I came top in Latin. And we're starting chemistry next term. I'm the only one who's done it before.'

'That's good.' She wasn't quite sure what Latin and chemistry were.

'I suppose you'll be going to the girls' grammar school next year?'

'I don't know if I can. I'd have to win a scholarship first.'

As the older boys and girls gathered in chattering clusters and the adults bent their heads over the map, she was glad again to have someone her own age to talk to, even if he did seem to know so much more than she did.

They started off down a cart-track. Edie fell into step beside Denis. For once Nonny hung back in the rear, without enthusiasm. They could see the grey buildings of a farm halfway up the opposite hillside. They crossed a ford, and then they were climbing steadily. The ruts of the track gave way to churned mud and an iron gate barred the entrance to the farmyard. The leading ramblers halted here, and looked round for Clifford.

'Do you think we should ask permission to go through?' said Mrs Crabtree.

'Get away. It's a public footpath,' Clifford told her. 'They can't stop us. As long as we shut all the gates behind us.'

The yard gate swung open unwillingly under his hand. As they streamed through, a collie rushed at them, barking furiously.

Edie always felt uneasy about walking through someone else's property. It felt like trespassing. It was different on the open hills. She could never make herself believe that the mountains belonged to just one person. Now, with the grey farm walls closing round her and an iron gate barring the way, she sensed eyes watching her from the shut windows. As the ramblers trooped through the gate and closed it behind them, she felt they were exercising in a prison yard.

The fear sprang suddenly into reality as there was an angry banging on the farmhouse window. Behind the glass they could see a woman's face shouting at them.

The Crabtrees stopped uncertainly.

'Should I go and have a word with her?' Mr Crabtree asked.

'Best not,' Clifford warned him. 'You'll only get the rough side of her tongue, by the sound of it. We're not doing any harm. The quicker we're out of sight, the better. She's happen had twenty parties through here already today.'

His smile struggled for mastery over his face. He waved to the woman.

'Good day to you, missus. Don't you worry. We'll not leave the gate unfastened.'

On the far side of the yard, where the track opened out into the fields, a second gate was tied up with rope. Denis ran forward and sprang on to the second rail, preparing to vault over. But Clifford Ramsden bellowed after him, 'Get off that gate, you silly beggar! You'll have half the gates in Derbyshire off their hinges, showing off like that. It's small wonder we've no friends left amongst the farmers, if lads like you don't know how to carry on in the countryside.'

Edie felt her insides curl up in horror. If she had been scolded like that in front of the whole group, she would have wanted a little hole to open in front of her, down which she could crawl and never come out again.

Denis's face went bright red. With a muttered 'Sorry,' he dropped to the ground and waited sullenly, as Clifford untied the gate and the ramblers trooped through. His mother whispered furiously to him as she passed. Edie hung back till the last, and held the gate as her father tied it up again.

Denis did not speak until Clifford strode off again to the head of the line. Then he burst out, 'Did he have to do that? I only weigh six stone. I wouldn't have hurt his rotten old gate.'

It was Edie Ramsden's turn to be shocked. 'But we never do that! It's like dropping orange peel. Or leaving gates open. A proper rambler never climbs gates.'

'Thanks for nothing! If you're going to be holier-than-thou, you should have stayed in your old Sunday School!'

He looked as if she had smacked him across the face. He walked off quickly ahead of her, avoiding his parents. Edie was left alone. Nonny caught her up and saw her face. His own scowl softened and he tried to raise a grin for her.

'Cheer up, our Edie. You were in the right. He's got a lot to learn yet, little know-all. They'll not call us hooligans, just because we come from the towns.'

It didn't help. Edie knew she was right. Her father had taught her well. But she had found a new friend, and now she had lost him already. Miserably she followed her father.

The path had disappeared in the short sheep-cropped grass of the intake fields. They found themselves on the top of the cloud-swept hill, surrounded by stone walls. Clifford looked slowly round with the wind blowing through his hair.

'Should be a stile over this wall. It's marked as a footpath on the map.'

'I bet that map's twenty years old,' said Nonny. 'Look at it! It's been folded so many times, you could spit through the cracks without wetting it.'

'But I swear I walked this two years ago, and there was a stile then. A footpath's a footpath. You can't take it away.'

'They can, you know. Easy as winking. Take out the step, put two, three good stones in the gap, and a stile's a fence. Who's to know the difference?'

'Do we climb over it?' Mrs Crabtree asked.

'There's a good place here.' Nonny was already scrambling up the wall.

'You watch it!' Clifford called after him. 'If we have those stones down, they'll be after us for criminal damage.'

'Fair's fair, this time. Somebody should be after them, for closing a footpath.'

'Are you sure this is the place?' Mr Crabtree asked. 'Or had we better go back?'

'I'll not be turned back again. Not after last week. Look, there's the map. You can see for yourself. Public right of way. A farmer can have title deeds as old as Domesday, but they can't gainsay a right of way.'

'You and your maps!' grinned Nonny, from the top of the wall. 'When they come to bury you, I'll put one in your coffin marked *Pearly Gates: latitude 91 degrees north, longitude 181 degrees west, height 1,000 miles.*'

'Yes, and if you read your New Testament you'll find there's a public right of way up to Heaven, and all!' Clifford joked back. 'Right, girls, are you fit? Mind the drop on the other side. It's a bit steepish.'

Clifford caught Edie safely under the armpits as she jumped down. The next field fell away in a long, sharp slope, with a grey thread of road at the bottom and a single car chugging round the side of the hill. Now she could run, had to run, because the hill was too steep for her to keep her balance any other way. The wind streamed through her hair and her skirt flew out behind her; it felt like flying.

'I wish I could still do that,' Mrs Crabtree called, as Edie tore past her.

The field levelled out and tufts of bulrushes warned of boggy ground, and another stone wall stood between her and the road. They climbed over. Denis still wouldn't look round.

'Told you so!' Clifford called triumphantly from the other side of the road. 'Who said there wasn't a path across here?'

'Is that it?' Mrs Crabtree looked doubtfully down at her bare legs above her ankle socks. 'It doesn't look very inviting.' Leading away from the road there was a dark tunnel between two hedges. It was filled with rank weeds and nettles. 'Are you sure this is the right way?'

Even Clifford sounded less confident. 'This used to be a picture in spring. I've seen it when these banks were a mass of violets. But it's the way, all right. It will take us down to the river at Cowgill Force. We can catch the bus back from Stoneyheugh Bridge.'

'It's about time someone walked it, by the look of it.' Denis's father cut at the nearest nettle with his walking stick. 'Unless there's another path.'

'Not unless you want to walk all the way round by road.'

'Walking sticks to the fore!' called Mr Crabtree.

The youngsters scorned walking sticks. But the Crabtrees carried them. They set off down the leafy lane, beating down the nettles and trampling them under their boots. Edie kept close behind her father, avoiding Denis. The shadows were chilly and mud squelched underfoot. Brambles crept like trip-wires through the grass and groped out of hedges to scratch unwary faces and tangle in knitted jumpers.

The chatter became subdued. It was hard work picking their way down the unfriendly path. Edie felt small again, hemmed in between tall figures in front and behind. She peered ahead for a glimpse of Denis, but she couldn't see him now.

As the lane dropped lower, the water began to lie in boggy pools across their path.

'Hey! I think Clifford's got river mixed up with road,' Annie Burton shouted from the back. 'You didn't tell us we'd to bring our bathing costumes.'

'It's a path, all right. And if you don't walk it, you'll lose it, like the rest. Don't you fret, Annie. You'll not mistake the river when we get to it. I haven't brought you down here for nothing. Hey up. What's this?'

Around the next bend, where the beech trees spread dark branches over their heads, was an iron gate, padlocked. The rails were criss-crossed with barbed wire. Beyond it, a wood sloped brown and damp and deeply shadowed. Edie stood still. All round her the splashing footsteps stopped. She could hear the deep, booming rush of water through the silence that had fallen over the group. But she could see nothing inside the gate except a massive tangle of dark trees and brambles. The waterfall must be deep in that wood, out of sight, and now out of reach. She found that she did not want to go on. In the half-darkness, the silent, padlocked gate made her uneasy.

'Looks like that's it. The beggars have beaten us again,' Clifford said wearily.

But Nonny was already plunging his hand into his rucksack.

'Oh, no, they haven't! I've brought a pair of wire-cutters this time.'

'Take more than wire-cutters to get through that padlock. Let alone what's beyond. A flame-thrower'd be more like it.'

'Well, we can all climb gates. Young Denis needn't think he's the only one that knows how.'

Edie winced. Denis must have heard that.

Clifford looked at Mr and Mrs Crabtree, at Annie Burton and her friends, at the thin-faced boys in their first year out of school, at Edie. He shook his head.

'Save that for tomorrow, lad. It could mean trouble,' Clifford told him. 'There's youngsters here that don't even know what it's all about . . . Right, Annie!' he called to the back of the line. 'Looks as if you're in the lead, after all. You'll have to put your best foot forward, though. It's a heck of a long way round by road, if you want to get the bus home for tea-time.'

A cloud of anger descended on Nonny's face, but no one else argued. A gloom had settled over the company. They picked their way back, over the flattened nettles and the water-filled prints of their own boots.

As they sorted themselves out into a straggling line, Edie found with a start that she was walking beside Denis again. A quick glance sideways at his face told her that he had not meant to be there. He was staring ahead, his expression tight with dislike. Crowded in by the overgrown hedges, they could not escape from each other. She tried a nervous smile.

'Will your father write about this for his newspaper? Will he tell people what the landowners are doing?'

'Oh, yes! I can just see it on the posters outside the newsagents! *Youth Club Driven Back by Massed Ranks of Stinging Nettles*. I suppose you think that's going to make my father star reporter on the *Exchange and Echo*?'

She could not stop the flare of sudden anger. His words stung like the nettles.

'But it's important! They won't let people like us walk anywhere!'

He did not bother to answer.

Edie was glad when they stepped out on to the road again. She lifted her face to the open hills, feeling the sharp edge of the wind graze her cheeks. She had forgotten that the torn grey clouds would still be blowing across the sky and their shadows racing over the fields.

Nonny drew a deep breath, sharing her feeling.

'That does it. That's the last time I mess about in country lanes. I'm going back to the hills tomorrow.'

They began to swing more vigorously down the metalled road, with the clash of their hobnailed boots carrying them along. They did not like the road, but at least it was open walking. A flight of cyclists sped round the bend behind them, crying a greeting as they swooped past.

'Who's going to give us a song?' called Mrs Crabtree.

'I will!' From the front, Nonny Rees's voice rose clearly in a tune that Edie had never heard before.

'I'm a rambler, I'm a rambler, from Manchester way.
I get all my pleasure the hard moorland way.
I may be a wage-slave on Monday,
But I am a free man on Sunday.'

The others swung along in silence until he had finished. No one else knew the song either.

'That's a new one on me,' said Clifford. 'Is there any more to it?'

Nonny looked over his shoulder and grinned.

'Aye. And it's still being written. Listen.

'There's pleasure in dragging through peat bogs and bragging
Of all the fine walks that you know;
There's even a measure of some kind of pleasure
In wading through ten feet of snow.
I've stood on the edge of the Downfall,
And seen all the valleys outspread,
And sooner than part from the mountains,
I think I would rather be dead.'

This time they all joined in the chorus.

'I'm a rambler, I'm a rambler from Manchester way,
I get all my pleasure the hard moorland way.
I may be a wage-slave on Monday,
But I am a free man on Sunday.'

'A free man on Sunday?' Edie's father smiled, savouring the words. 'I like the sound of that!'

'That's silly,' muttered Denis, still cross. 'Your club doesn't go rambling on a Sunday.'

'Nonny does!' Edie said hotly. '*And* my dad does.' In her irritation she found herself talking as though he had done it all his life, instead of once. 'There's a group called Red Grouse. They take wire-cutters. And they pull up any notices that say *Trespassers Will Be Prosecuted* where it should be a public footpath. And they climb to the tops of the hills, even if they haven't got a permit.'

'Do they *really*?' Denis's eyes were sparkling suddenly behind his glasses as he swung round. He seemed to have forgotten they were enemies. 'You never said. Do you think they'd take me?'

Without waiting for an answer he ran to the front of the line. She saw him catch hold of Nonny's elbow.

A wave of jealous fury swept through Edie. All day, the same thought had been eating into her mind. Sunday. The way her father had described it to her. All Sunday in the hills. But she couldn't, could she?

Chapter 13

'You've got the wrong day,' Bobby said.

Edith jumped. She had thought Bobby was asleep. But there were two round dark eyes peeping at her above the sheet.

'You mind your own business,' she said, pulling on her Fair Isle jumper over the tartan skirt she wore on Saturdays. She stood in front of the mirror, dragging her hairbrush through the tight Sunday curls, beating and flattening them till they began to collapse at last into the plain, straight locks of her Saturday self.

'What's the matter with your best frock? Have you ripped it? Mum'll murder you.'

'Ask me no questions and I'll tell you no lies.'

She glanced out of the window, and her heart sank a little lower. The morning was grey and threatened rain. It was harder to be brave when the sun was not shining. And then the treacherous thought came into her mind that if it rained hard, her father would not have taken her rambling, even on a Saturday.

She tiptoed downstairs. She was still wearing her slippers, because her boots were in the kitchen. The slippers were soft and cosy, a last, safe bit of her usual Sunday self that she could still cling to for a little while longer.

She opened the door. Her mother was in the back room, laying the table. She looked up as Edie entered. A puzzled frown held her face for a moment, as she stared at her daughter. And then she laughed.

'You're a day out. You'll be wanting a four-day week

next, with two Saturdays in a row! What are you doing in that old jumper and skirt? You want your best frock on.'

Edie picked up her boots and gripped them firmly to give herself courage.

'I'm going with Dad.'

Clifford came in from the yard and Maggie whipped round on him.

'Now see what you've done! Here's our Edie saying she's going rambling with you. I've told you no good would come of it. That Nonny Rees!'

'Don't blame Nonny.'

'He's got wild friends. You'll be leading our Edie into trouble. Look at her! Standing there with her boots in her hand like a lad. She'll be wanting a pair of shorts and a rucksack next.'

'Aye, and why shouldn't she? There's plenty of other lasses do.'

Edie felt suddenly like a rag doll that two children are fighting over. She wanted to shout at them, Stop it, both of you!

But her father put his hands on her shoulders, warm and firm. He smiled down at her with that special smile that made her heart turn over. Did that mean he was going to take her? Then his voice spoke, slow and very seriously.

'Listen, Edie. Your mother's right. I'll not take you on Sunday. And do you know why? You've seen those books in the front room. Sunday School prizes. Inside every one there's the same thing written: *Clifford Ramsden. Never absent, never late. Oldway Methodist Sunday School.* It's that that's made me the man I am. Your mother may think I've changed, but I haven't. I'm not missing chapel just for the feel of the wind on my face. There's a fight to be fought now, and I'll not turn back from it.'

'Then I want to fight too.'

His freckled face crinkled with laughter.

'Aye! But I reckon we'll still have a few battles left for you by the time you leave Sunday School. I shouldn't think we'll have finished putting the world to rights so soon!'

Maggie turned away and broke more eggs into the frying pan. Edie bit her lip and tried to smile at her father. She was aware of an enormous relief washing through her. She had tried to go, and failed. Now she could stay safe inside the familiar pattern. She was not being given the chance to strip off the habit of a lifetime. She would not have to face the gamekeepers with their guns and dogs. She would not have to go to school tomorrow and answer the curious questions from Jimmy Greenwood and Mary Bassett about where she had been. She would not have to pass Miss Lancaster's house and think about going to hell.

'I'll cut your sandwiches,' she offered.

She put a neat stack of bread and potted meat in his snap tin, and handed it across the table. Her mother turned, snatched the tin from her and opened it.

'Give over,' Clifford protested. 'The lass has done them for me. She's on my side, even if you aren't.'

Margaret Ramsden stalked to the larder. She took out a large new fruit cake and cut a slab off it. Edie stared at it in astonishment. There was always a new cake baked for Sunday tea. It was cooked on Saturday morning and put in a special tin, whole and untouched till tea-time on Sunday. Not once in her life had Edie seen her mother cut that cake on Sunday morning.

Without a word, Maggie fitted the slab of cake neatly beside the sandwiches and snapped the lid shut. She handed the box to Clifford.

He stood up and put an arm round each of their shoulders.

'I'm a lucky man,' he said gruffly. 'I've got two good lasses. I wish I could take both of you with me.'

'Edie's coming to chapel with me.'

'I know. That's where I want her.'

Maggie spoke briskly. 'And you mind what you get up to.'

'I won't let you down. I'll be back in time for chapel at half past six.'

A minute later, he had picked up his rucksack and walking stick and was gone. The room, which he had filled with his presence, grew suddenly colder. Edie watched her mother's busy movements fall still and saw her shrink within herself.

She looked small and lonely. Is this what growing up is? wondered Edie. Seeing the same people, but differently.

She fingered the fork in front of her.

'Is it *very* bad not to go to chapel? Mr Sutcliffe seemed to think it was all right, so long as Dad was back for evening service.'

'I didn't marry John Sutcliffe. And you can tell Bobby if he's not down in five minutes he'll go without breakfast. At this rate, they'll be short of four Ramsdens instead of one!'

But her father was not the only one missing from chapel. Denis Crabtree was not there. He wasn't in Sunday School either. She knew what that meant. They had taken Denis, and left her behind.

Chapter 14

The ridge was straight ahead of Denis. Only Nonny was in front of him, going for the top as though his legs were piston rods instead of flesh and blood.

Denis was panting painfully. His glasses kept slipping as the sweat ran down his nose. But apart from that he was doing well. So much for Clifford Ramsden, who hadn't wanted him to come. He'd show them.

Rocks and brown heather on his left. To his right, a green hollow. Easier walking.

'Look out!' Clifford's warning shout rang from below.

He looked above him. Nonny had stopped too, close under the summit. The older boy turned and began to run, straight for the crest. Denis swung round. What had he seen?

Two men and a dog. Coming hard and fast up the side of the ridge. He started to run uphill after Nonny. More yells from below. He couldn't hear what they were saying. The blood was pounding in his ears and gasps were torn from his chest. He had a glimpse of Red Grouse racing to outstrip the keepers.

Another head, coming over the skyline on his left in silhouette. Terrifyingly close this time. He sprinted right. Springing green grass underfoot. Spongy moss. He must make it to the summit. Can't let Nonny down. Forget the keeper. What's Lil yelling? Better ignore it. Keep going.

Squelch. The cold shock as his leg plunged down into liquid mud. Dragging at it desperately. Hands clutching at tufts of bulrushes he hadn't noticed. Idiot! He couldn't move.

Lil shouted again, 'Nonny! Help Denis!'

Denis shut his eyes. 'No! Don't, Nonny! You've got to get to the top. Never mind about me.'

He opened them again. The keeper had stopped on the edge of the treacherous moss. He was watching, stick in hand.

Nonny was scrambling down the side of the hill as fast as he could, yelling at him.

'Get over to your left. Lean your weight on that tussock. Can you get your knee out now? Stand up. Now, jump across to the next one. Flaming little townee! Couldn't you see the bog cotton in front of your nose?'

Bog cotton? Little wisps like cotton wool, on spiky reed stems. All round him. The glint of water oozing over black peat between the moss.

Everyone was watching him now. The rest of Red Grouse had come over the lip of the hollow and stopped sullenly. The first two keepers were close behind them. Only the dog looked cheerful as it moved round to pen the trespassers like sheep.

Denis stepped forward. Leaped. Slipped, and jumped again. Nonny's harsh voice was calling out instructions. The wind cut through his wet clothes like a sharp knife.

The last leap. Nonny's strong hand grasping his, dragging him back to safety. He stumbled on to his hands and knees in the mud. Two boots in front of him. Gaiters. Tweed knickerbockers. A knobbed stick. He raised himself up and looked into the hard blue of the keeper's eyes. The man grinned down at him without warmth.

'Right, my lad! So that's your game, is it? Thought you'd outrun me. Fancied a long hike over the grouse moors, did you? Well, this time, you're going to get more than you bargained for. March!'

Chapter 15

Clifford was not on the early bus. At quarter to five Edie began to lay the table for tea. It seemed strange to be setting it in the kitchen. Sunday tea had always meant sandwiches and cake in the front room, sitting around the fire. But her father could not manage a plate of roast lamb with gravy balanced on his knees. All the same, she got out the best pink and white china and set it on the lace-edged cloth. Then she cut a plate of paste sandwiches and arranged them in a neat pyramid in the centre of the table. Bobby eyed them hungrily.

At five o'clock he said, 'Can we start? I'm starving.'

'You'll start when your father comes, and not before,' ordered Maggie.

The hands of the clock moved round to ten past five. Bobby kept his eyes fixed on the mound of pink and white triangles as though he was afraid they would run away if he did not watch them. Maggie's glance kept darting towards the clock.

'You're missing *Children's Hour*,' she said.

Edie turned on the wireless. But the serial had already started and her mind could not make sense of what was happening. Besides, she was listening for something else.

'He's coming!' she cried at last, running to the window.

But the footsteps went on down the alley.

At twenty to six, Maggie said, 'I'll mash the tea. The next bus will be in any minute.'

But the tea was mashed and the pot filled, and still he did not come. With a sudden movement, Maggie picked up the teapot and carried it to the table.

'Well, come on, then. Don't just sit there staring at it.'

'Hooray!' Bobby gabbled his grace and grabbed for the first sandwich. It was gone in two gulps.

'Go easy!' said his mother. 'There's other folk want some besides you. Like pigs with cherries, you are.'

But Edie found she had no appetite.

By six o'clock the washing-up was done. Edie had brought her father's shoes down and put them in the kitchen, ready polished. His suit was laid out on the bed. Already footsteps were going up the street on the way to chapel. Maggie Ramsden put on her Sunday coat and hat. She turned out the gas under the saucepan, where Clifford's plate of dinner had been keeping warm in the steam.

'If he comes now, he'll have to go without his tea.'

The clock in the front room chimed quarter past six. Edie felt sick with betrayal. Her father had said he would be back in time for chapel. He had let them down. Her warm, safe world was crumbling. Nonny and Red Grouse were taking him away from her.

She glanced anxiously at her mother, aware that she was the nearest target for Maggie's hurt. Maggie took out her long hat pin and laid it down again.

'That's it, then. He's missed that bus as well.'

'Why don't you go?' Edie thought silently. 'If you don't hurry, you'll be late too.'

Maggie picked up her Sunday gloves and studied her face in the mirror. The line of her mouth was not quite firm. Still she did not go to the door.

Edie stared at her in dumb agony. She wanted to cry out, Aren't you going to chapel either? A childish voice inside her was pleading. You *must* go. Something must stay the same today. It's bad enough that Dad hasn't come home and we don't know where he is; and Miss Lancaster says if you don't go to chapel you go to hell. But he's a man, and everyone knows that men are weak and sinful. They drink or gamble or get into fights. Dad doesn't do that, so it has to be trespassing. But you're my *mother*. Women like you have got to be strong and brave, whatever happens. My whole world would fall apart if you changed too.

Maggie swung round from the mirror and said crisply to Edie, 'Well, don't stare at me like a ninny! Whatever's happened to him, sitting here twiddling my thumbs isn't going to mend it. You see that Bobby's in bed before I get back.'

She snatched up her handbag from the hall table. The front door closed and her heels went clipping briskly up the street towards Oldway Chapel.

'Whatever's happened to him...?' Slowly the words sank in. Edie found herself staring at the shut door, wide-eyed.

Bobby did not want to go to bed before his father came home. But at last he went sulkily upstairs, and the house was quiet. Edie spread out a jigsaw on the floor. But she was too worried to start it. It seemed strange and wrong to be sitting in the kitchen on a Sunday, with the front room growing cold and unused. Edie fingered the pieces of jigsaw, but all the time she was listening for footsteps in the alley outside the yard.

In less than two hours, Maggie was home. She took one look at the empty kitchen and the dinner-plate still sitting over the cold saucepan.

'He's not back, then?'

Edie shook her head silently. She was too scared to speak her thoughts aloud. When her mother had come down from kissing Bobby goodnight she began to knit.

It was ten past nine when they heard the yard gate open. Edie's eyes flew to her mother's face. The needles stopped. The wool hung poised over the half-made stitch. Then Maggie's fingers began flying furiously again.

'He'll be traipsing mud all over my kitchen now.'

But Clifford tiptoed through the back door with his boots in his hand. He smiled at them guiltily, like a small boy.

'I'm sorry,' he said. 'Have you been waiting on me?'

'Oh, no!' Maggie retorted. 'Nobody's been waiting on you. We've been to Scarborough Fair, we have. We didn't even notice you were missing. You great chump! Of course we've been waiting for you, since five o'clock. Where have you been?'

'Halfway to Sheffield, by the feel of it. Did they miss me at chapel?'

'I shouldn't think there were above forty people asked me where you were, starting with John Sutcliffe. A fine fool I felt, when I didn't even know myself! That Mrs Greenwood; the way she spoke, you'd think it was grounds for divorce, going to chapel without your husband two weeks running. Though I notice her Bert's still at home with his bad chest.'

'I'm sorry, love! I didn't mean to leave you at the sharp end. Flaming keepers . . .'

At the sound of his father's voice, Bobby came running down the stairs in his bare feet.

'Is it Dad? Is he back?' He stopped in the doorway, and then ran across and caught hold of his father's hand. 'You've got blood on you! Did the keepers have guns today? Did they shoot you?'

Clifford rumpled his hair. 'Not them! You've been reading too many cowboy comics. I had an argument with a bit of barbed wire crossing a brook, that's all. They had great sticks, though, with knobs on. And they'd have used those on us if we'd made trouble. Three of them, there were, this time. And a dog. They meant business, too. They drove us like sheep, the beggars. Right over the other side, into Edale. Every time we tried to head back the way we came, they cut us off. I thought Lil was going to go for them once, she was that mad. But they turned nasty. Even she saw sense.

'They must have driven us ten miles out of our way. And when they left us on the Sheffield road, they were laughing fit to bust. They knew we'd got return tickets from Hayfield and we'd not be able to use them there. Most of those kids didn't have enough money for the bus home. They'll be walking yet.'

'Serves them right. You should write for a permit if you want to go on those moors.'

'Nay. It seems wrong to me that you have to have a piece of paper before you can climb a hill or look at a waterfall. The daft thing is that they drove us miles across their flaming grouse moor. We'd have done a lot less damage if they'd just left us alone. I'm sorry, lass. I never thought I wouldn't be back for half past six.'

'I knew you wouldn't. You went looking for trouble, and you got it.'

'Nay, Maggie. That's not right.'

'Those friends of Nonny's want a fight, even if you don't. And they'll get one, the way you're carrying on now. If you keep in with them, you'll end up in prison, you mark my words.'

Prison. The bitter, black word sank into Edie. Bobby's mouth went as round as a small red cherry.

Maggie got up briskly. 'Your tea's cold. And the meat will be as dry as old shoe leather. And you get back into bed, our Bobby, before you catch your death of cold.'

Clifford lifted Bobby on to his knee. 'I'm that hungry, I could eat cold kale and candle-grease. And I'll tell you something else, our Bobby. All day I've been looking across at Kinder Scout. And there's words been going through my head. *I will lift up mine eyes unto the hills, from whence cometh my help. My help cometh from the Lord, who made heaven and earth.* One day, I said to myself, I'm going to take our Edie and Bobby by the hand, and the three of us are going to stand on top of that mountain.'

'Bobby's too small,' said Edie in a flash of jealousy.

He looked at her gravely. 'Stand over there . . . Aye, I thought so. You've a bit of growing to do yourself, yet!' And he hugged Bobby and kissed him goodnight.

The thought that had tormented Edie all day would not be held back any longer.

'Was Denis Crabtree there?'

'Who? Oh, you mean the reporter's son. Yes, he was. I tried to talk him out of it, but he was set on coming. I'd have been home sooner, only I had to take him round to his parents first. I'd some explaining to do and all, seeing as he'd fallen in a bog running away from the keepers. It turns out he hadn't told his parents what we'd be up to, so they weren't best pleased with him or with me, bringing him home so late in that state! And he's still not best friends with me either, after the way I called him yesterday over that gate.

'Still, he's a plucky little lad. He must have been fair dropping by the time we reached that bus, and wet through with mud. But he never complained. He may look a weak little chap with his skinny legs and his glasses, but he's got guts. I'll say that for him.'

It was too much for Edie.

'It's not fair! You took Denis Crabtree on a Sunday, but you wouldn't take *me*!' she cried.

And she ran from the room, upstairs to bed.

Chapter 16

There was a furious rapping at the door. Edie's father, sitting at the tea-table in his Monday working clothes, dropped his knife and fork.

'I'll go?' offered Edie. But she let the words hang uncertainly in the air, like a question.

'No, I'd better, by the sound of it,' said her mother. 'You'd think there'd been a death in the street, hammering on the door like that.'

But she had not reached the door before it burst open, and Nonny Rees pushed past her, waving the local paper at Clifford. His face was red with anger.

'Have you seen tonight's *Exchange and Echo*?'

'Have I, fiddle. You should know better than to ask. I don't waste hard-earned money on a rag like that.'

'Look here! Page four. Just you listen to this!

Red Grouse, an aptly-named Communist sports group consisting mostly of unemployed youths, provoked a confrontation yesterday with the forces of law and order. Three gamekeepers, employed by Mr Arthur Headingley of Oakleigh Hall, found themselves face to face with a group of twelve, trespassing in the middle of his grouse moor. But we are happy to say that the hooligans came off worst. Although they outnumbered the keepers four to one, the young townees took to their heels and fled. We hope that a long trek home from the wrong side of the county will have given them time to think about their irresponsible actions.

This kind of trespassing on private property, which all

respectable rambling clubs condemn, has become an increasing nuisance in recent years. We understand that the young law-breakers were accompanied by Clifford Ramsden, a well-known local trade unionist, who, in our opinion, might have been expected to know better.'

'There! What did I tell you?' exclaimed Maggie. 'You see where your Sabbath-breaking's got you? They've put you down for a Communist, now.'

'Nay, Maggie. Folk round here know me,' Clifford protested. 'I've always been Labour and chapel. There's no one'll believe that.'

'Won't they?' Maggie asked him. 'Won't they? There's even some at chapel'd be glad to believe it. Give me that paper. That editor! I'd like to give him a piece of my mind!'

'It's the way he laughs at us,' grated Nonny. 'There were only eleven of us, and a kid. And they had a shotgun and sticks. What did he expect us to do? Have a stand-up fight? I tell you, Clifford, there weren't enough of us. We'll never do anything until we join together. We need to get all the ramblers. Hundreds and hundreds of us. They'd never stop us then, no matter how many of them there were. We could even get to the top of Kinder Scout.'

'You'd be breaking the law. I've told you. You'll end up in prison one of these days,' Maggie warned him.

'Maybe we've got to, and all,' Nonny challenged her. 'If that's the only way to make the rest of the country sit up and listen to us. It shouldn't be a crime to climb a mountain!'

Edie stared down at the newspaper lying on the kitchen table. Getting your name in the paper was supposed to be something to boast about. Like the time last year when she had recited a poem at the Sunday School Anniversary. Or when she and Bobby had been listed among the mourners at Grandad's funeral. But not this. Not words like "hooligans". Clifford Ramsden? The father she had been so proud of?

'Who gave them the story? That's what I want to know,' Nonny cried. 'It wasn't the keepers. There isn't one of their names there, only ours.'

'Mine,' said Clifford drily. 'I notice they've not printed yours or Lil's.'

'But which of Red Grouse would write a flaming daft thing like that? Making us out to look like a bunch of idiots. There isn't one of them would rat on us.'

Edie's eyes met her father's. She made herself say it before he did.

'Denis Crabtree was there.'

'Get away. He's only a kid.'

Edie had difficulty keeping her voice steady. 'You've forgotten. His father's a newspaper reporter. On the *Exchange and Echo*. And you said they were cross with you last night.'

Nonny's fist slammed down on the table. 'Of course! You wait till I get my hands on him. The little rat! And his la-di-da father! That's the last time they come rambling with us! I'm going round to see them now and give them a piece of my mind!'

'Now steady on,' Clifford said reasonably. 'Give the lad a fair trial. We don't know for a fact that it was him.'

But Edie turned away, sickened. She knew that Nonny was right. Denis had not forgiven Clifford for that scolding. He had got his own back now, and Mr Crabtree had got his story.

The door crashed shut behind Nonny.

Chapter 17

'Your father's a Commie.'

'He's not!'

'He is. Red Ramsden!'

Jimmy Greenwood was facing her, legs apart, blocking her way down the school hill. More boys and girls from her class were streaming past on their way out of school, turning their heads to listen, crowding round. Edie looked out desperately over their heads at the grey smoke haze hanging above the chimneys of the town. She wanted to take to her heels and run down the steep pavement, to feel her heels flying up under her skirt and the wind in her hair as she had felt them that far-away Saturday when she and Denis had raced across the hills.

But she could not. She was hemmed in. Jimmy Greenwood was grinning at her, a broader and bolder grin than his mother's sly smile on the chapel steps. He was not going to let her go yet. She still did not know what a Communist was, but the way people said it made it sound as though it was the worst thing anyone could be. But her father had said that Red Grouse were grand young people. And anyway, it wasn't true, what the papers had said about him.

'Bolshie! Commie!'

'He's not! He's in the Labour Party.'

'He's a Red. Our mam says so. He doesn't come to chapel now, does he? Him and Nonny Rees. It was in the papers. Everyone knows he's a Commie.'

'My dad *does* go to chapel! How dare you say that!'

'Oh! Miss Hoity-Toity! Well, he wasn't there last Sunday, was he?'

'Yes, he was! He meant to! He missed the bus. It wasn't *his* fault!'

'Told you so. He's stopped coming, hasn't he? Two weeks now. That shows he's a Commie. They don't believe in God.'

'He does!' That much she was certain of.

'Doesn't have to be a Commie, just because he doesn't go to chapel,' sneered Mary Bassett at Edie's side. 'You don't know everything, Jimmy Greenwood. There's lots of people don't go to church who aren't Communists. He's just an atheist, isn't he, Edie?'

'He's not! He's not!' Edie cried in desperation between them.

'If you're an atheist, you go to hell. That's what Miss Lancaster said at Sunday School.'

'Commies go to hell, and all,' shouted Jimmy. 'So there!'

'Shut up!' yelled Edie at both of them. 'He's *not* an atheist. And he's not a Communist. And even if he was, he'd be better than your father!'

'Miss Lancaster said we ought to pray for people who don't go to chapel,' said Mary. 'She thinks you're in great moral danger, living in a family like yours, Edie Ramsden. She said we all ought to be specially nice to you and talk to you about Jesus, because it might be too late to save your father, but we could still save you and your Bobby if we prayed hard . . .'

Edie swung round. Jimmy Greenwood was forgotten. Talk of Jesus had silenced him. But Mary Bassett had a sharp white face with freckles, and a crop of red hair. She sat next to Edie in Sunday School, and pinched her when Miss Lancaster wasn't looking.

'Miss Lancaster never said that. I was in Sunday School too.'

'Yes, she did. When you were putting the hymn books away. She called us all round and whispered it. That's true, isn't it, Shirley? And I've been praying for you ever since.'

'They'll leave the rest of us to fight their battles nearer home,' her mother had said. Edie's fist shot out and collided with Mary Bassett's eye.

'Well, you can pray for somebody else! My dad's worth ten of yours! Mr Sutcliffe says so, and he's the minister. And he does go to chapel. He does! He does!'

With each word her fists were flying out. Mary grabbed her by the hair with one hand and punched her in the chest with the other. She was the stronger of the two. Edie doubled over with the breath knocked out of her.

'Come on, Mary! Come on, Mary! Belt her one!'

The little ones scurried homeward, frightened, but the bigger boys and girls crowded round shouting and cheering. Edie dared not back down now. She was fighting for her father's honour. She wrenched her head out of Mary's clutch, feeling the hair torn up by its roots, and stormed in again with her fists. Mary went reeling back, blood spurting shockingly from her nose over her white collar. She was maddened now. She came charging back, kicking and punching at the same time. With the sudden pain in her shin, Edie hardly noticed the blow on her eye, but the world went black for a moment.

The sky cleared, but only for an instant. Darkness, like a great thundercloud, seemed to descend over Mary's red hair. There was a fierce grip on Edie's shoulder, forcing the two girls apart.

It was the great, grey-suited bulk of Mr Holmshaw, their headmaster.

'What do you think you're doing! Fighting in the street like drunken navvies? Two *girls*! It's disgraceful!'

He turned on the ring of children that was already backing away from him.

'Get home, all of you!' he bellowed. 'If there's one child left outside these gates in sixty seconds, I'll have that boy or girl into my room and they'll not sit down for a week. You ought to be ashamed of yourselves, watching such a disgusting exhibition.'

The street cleared, like a slate wiped clean. They knew Mr Holmshaw meant every word.

'Gor! You'll cop it now!' gasped Jimmy Greenwood, as he took to his heels.

Edie put out her tongue at him. She dared not speak, with that grip still hard on her collar.

'Come in off this street at once,' said Mr Holmshaw, dragging them in through the gate. 'You're disgracing my school in front of the whole town.'

Inside the classroom he let go of them. Blood still ran from Mary's nose and she was sobbing into a scarlet-stained handkerchief. Edie watched her uneasily, not sure whether she was really hurt or trying to gain Mr Holmshaw's sympathy.

Mr Holmshaw did not seem to be moved by either blood or tears.

'Now then! Who started this? I want the culprit to own up.'

'She did!' spluttered Mary.

'She said rude things about my dad,' Edie answered defiantly. 'She said he was an atheist.'

'So that's it, is it?' Mr Holmshaw exclaimed. 'I might have guessed Clifford Ramsden was at the bottom of this. Like father, like daughter. So he's not content with stirring up trouble at the mill with his union meetings. Well, you can tell him from me I'll have no troublemakers in this school with your rights and your unions. In my school you'll do what you're told. I'll teach you to have respect for those above you. Hold out your hand.'

Edie felt the sudden shock of fear, even though, like every child in the school, she had known the penalty for fighting.

The cane was in the bottom of Mr Holmshaw's desk. He swished it lightly over his palm, and a fine powdering of chalk fanned through the air around him. Edie held out her hand, gripping it tightly round the wrist with the other. The two halves of her body were warring with each other, one to hold still, the other to pull away. Three times the cane came screaming through the air to bite her palm. Scalding tears were running down Edie's face when he finished. They were tears not just of pain, but of humiliation and a raging sense of injustice.

Then it was Mary's turn. One stroke only, because Edie had started it. But Mary screamed, and blood and tears bubbled faster into her handkerchief.

'Now, clean yourselves up and get along home. And that's the last time either of you will fight while you're in my school,' ordered Mr Holmshaw.

Seeing Mary make for the wash-basins, Edie wiped the tears from her face and ran for the gate. The school hill was deserted now. She could let herself fly at last, as she had wanted to half an hour ago. There was a healing joy in running that made the pain seem almost bearable. But there was still a bitter indignation inside her, a massive ache in her shin, and a smarting palm that she nursed against her side. Her face felt funny, too. Still, she reflected with satisfaction, she had probably won. She had not let herself cry out, even when she had been caned. And she had given Mary a bloody nose.

She stopped running before she reached the house, and opened the back door nervously.

Maggie Ramsden looked her up and down and wiped her hands on her apron.

'Looks like you've been in the wars,' she said carefully.

'I had a fight with Mary Bassett.'

'Oh, aye? Any particular reason?'

'They were saying rude things about Dad.'

'Like what?'

'Jimmy Greenwood said he was a Communist, and Mary Bassett said he was an atheist and he'll go to hell. But he won't, will he?'

'So that's what they're saying, is it? I shall have to see Mrs Bassett. Come here. I've no beefsteak to waste on that eye. You'll have to make do with cold water.'

She took Edie's hand. Edie let out a sharp gasp and pulled quickly away. But Maggie turned the palm over and looked at the fierce red stripes across it.

'Mary Bassett never did that,' she said quietly.

'No, Mr Holmshaw caught us. He gave me three, and Mary one.'

'Why's that? She's bigger than you.'

'Because I started it.'

'And she was calling your dad?'

'Yes.'

Maggie dipped a cloth in cold water and sponged Edie's swelling eye and throbbing palm.

'It's time I had a word with your father. You're getting more like him every day.'

'Is that bad?' Edie pushed the towel away from her face and looked up at her mother.

'Take that smile off your face, you cheeky monkey. Well, I suppose you're right. When I look around, I could have done a lot worse. Just think if I'd married Bert Greenwood! Would you fancy a boiled egg for your tea?'

Clifford Ramsden came home from work and stopped short in the doorway. Edie lifted her face proudly to him over the empty egg-shell.

'Oh, aye? And what does the other chap look like?'

'I made her nose bleed.'

'You did, did you? Let's have a proper look at you. By, that's a real shiner you've got there.'

'She's been fighting over you,' said Maggie. 'They're saying things at school.'

'Are they, now? Well, from what I've heard, I'd say she'd had the best of it.'

The proud smile he gave her made up for a lot of things.

Chapter 18

The queue wound all the way from the ticket barrier, round the station entrance and out on to the pavement. Hundreds of Saturday ramblers, waiting noisily for the trains that would take them out into the country for a few precious hours of freedom. Never mind that the day was overcast with a hint of rain in the wind. At least the rain would fall clean on the hills where they were going.

They were mostly young. Girls and boys, almost all of them in shorts. Checked shirts. Khaki jackets. And most with the canvas rucksacks that were their passport to adventure. Edie longed to have one of her own. To pack it full, with sandwiches, flask and spare clothing. To tuck her thumbs under the webbing straps. To swing it casually round in front of her and fish in the pockets for a map or a slab of chocolate. Even to complain laughingly about the weight as she shouldered it.

'There's Red Grouse!' Nonny ran across to join another group.

Edie looked enviously at the knot of girls and young men ahead of her. That girl with the short, curly hair must be Lil. She swung round to greet Nonny, and said something that made the rest of the group laugh uproariously. Those that were not on the dole had come straight from work. Only an hour ago, those heads had been bent over a loom, a machine bench, or a typewriter. Now they were bright-eyed with the promise of the weekend and freedom stretching ahead. Their knees showed pink above their woolly socks. Edie smoothed down her tartan skirt regretfully. One day, she would have her own shorts and rucksack.

Mrs Crabtree and Denis turned in under the station arch and Edie's stomach lurched. She noticed at once that Mr Crabtree was not with them. Good. That meant that he was too ashamed to face them. She was astonished to see her father waving the other two over as though nothing had happened. As though Mr Crabtree had never written that awful article about Red Grouse. She turned her back on them furiously. Denis should not have had the cheek to come, either.

Presently she was aware that someone was standing beside her. She would not look round.

'Hey!' Clifford nudged Edie. 'Denis is here. Aren't you going to say hullo?'

'I'm never going to speak to him as long as I live!'

She walked away to the front of the group.

'Edie!' Clifford strode after her. 'What's to do with you?'

'You saw the paper! You saw what they wrote about you. They *laughed* at you!'

'And you're going to blame the lad for that, without waiting to hear what he's got to say for himself?'

'Who else? He was there. Nonny said it was him.'

Clifford spoke seriously.

'Edie, there's only one Boss tells Ramsdens what's right and wrong. And it's not Nonny. Not even John Sutcliffe. At least give the lad a fair hearing . . .' He broke off as a buzz of excitement sent every head turning. 'Hey up! What's this?'

Two young men came through the station entrance, calling out to the queue. They had bundles of papers in their hands and they were giving them out to every rambler they passed.

'Support the Mass Trespass!'

'Climb Kinder Scout!'

'Strike a blow for the public right to the mountains!'

Edie felt a paper thrust into her own hand. She clutched it and looked down at the words.

If you love the mountains, join the Mass Trespass on Kinder Scout. This historic event will take place on Sunday, April 24th.

What do we want?

The freedom to sing as we walk.

The freedom to leave the path.

The freedom to climb the mountains.

What do the landowners want?

They'd like us to stay in the towns and keep the hills for themselves. But united, we cannot be turned back.

Rally starts at 2 p.m. at Hayfield Recreation Ground.

Free men and women everywhere, come and join us on the summit of Kinder Scout.

Kinder Scout. Always that name. All round her, the station was alive with noise. Groups of heads were bent over the leaflets. Some people laughed and threw them away. More read them, folded them up and put them away in their pockets. But there were some that began to talk eagerly amongst themselves. In the middle of Red Grouse, Lil was jumping up and down with excitement.

Nonny came running over waving a leaflet.

'How about it, Clifford? It's what we've always wanted! Hundreds of us, all bound for the top. They'll never stop us!'

Clifford laughed and shook his head.

'Steady on, lad. I'm a respectable family man, not one of you young tearaways. I won't say I haven't climbed Kinder Scout before now, because I'd be lying. But there's an art to trespassing, you know. You have to go canny-like. Just touch your cap to the gamekeeper if he catches you, and get him chatting to you about the grouse, friendly-like. Not like this! Shouting it across the whole country before you start. They'll have every man on the estates that can hold a stick or gun out waiting to get you.'

'We've tried your way. And look what happened. This time they'll never be able to stop all of us. There'll be hundreds of us spread out across the hillside. We'll get to the top. We'll *make* them change the law!'

'The law's on their side now. They'll have police in Hayfield waiting for you. Keepers on the hills. If there's trouble, you could land up in prison.'

'So what, if we're right? It's the only way to make them listen. Are you frightened?'

Clifford looked round at the eager boys and girls from Oldway watching him. He shrugged his shoulders with a wry grin.

'Don't look at this lot. I can just see Miss Lancaster's face if I took the whole youth club off and got them arrested. But on a Sunday afternoon, I'm a free man. I've just to follow my own conscience.'

He bent his head and read the leaflet again. In the stillness, Edith found her heart thumping in her chest. She didn't know what she wanted him to do. Then her father lifted his face, and his blue eyes were dancing with mischief.

'You're on!' he cried, clapping Nonny on the shoulder. 'We'll make them sit up and take notice of us, this time!'

The train let off an ear-splitting burst of steam. The platform gates clanged open and the crowd of passengers began to stream forward into the carriages.

The compartments were filling up fast. Clifford called to Edie to squeeze in beside him. But she shook her head.

'I like standing up.'

In the crowded corridor, she leaned against the window, staring out at the high brick wall and longing for it to give way to fields and woods.

'Did you get one of those leaflets about Kinder Scout?'

She came to with a shock. Denis was standing beside her. He gave her a half smile, that might have been either shyness or apology. This week, it was she who turned her head away. In spite of her father's words, her face felt frozen. She did not want to greet him.

'What's the matter with you today?'

'You told them!' she burst out, unable to hold the words back. 'You told your father how Red Grouse got chased off the moor. You made everybody laugh at him.'

'I didn't!'

'Don't pretend! I read it in the paper. Everybody must have read it. And your dad's not here today. That proves it. He daren't show his face to my dad and Nonny after what he wrote. If you had any shame, you'd have stayed at home too.'

'Home? Don't be daft. Dad's a reporter. He often has to work Saturday afternoons. If you must know, they've sent him to cover the Rugby League match, because the sports correspondent's got 'flu.' He grinned as he said it.

Edie paused. Some of the steam went out of her anger. Then the sight of Denis smiling, because he was right and she was wrong, made her crosser than ever.

'It doesn't matter! He still wrote that awful story. And you made him do it. You told lies about my dad because he told you off for climbing a gate.'

He gasped, as if she had hit him.

'You can't believe that! You're just as bad as Nonny. Do you think we don't want to climb the hills as much as you? All right, I told my dad what happened. And he wrote it up for the paper. But it was a *good* story. He wanted to tell people how you can't even step off the footpath without a permit. How the landowners want to keep the hills for themselves. How the gamekeepers chase working people off. But by the time the editor had got hold of it and printed it in his rotten paper, it came out all twisted and horrid. It's always the same here. Nothing Dad writes ends up the way he meant it to sound.'

'Then he shouldn't go on writing for it. The *Exchange and Echo*'s a rag. My dad wouldn't even *buy* it, let alone work for it.'

Denis sighed. 'Don't you start. You don't understand. Do you think my father *wanted* to leave the *Yorkshire Post*? He's a good reporter but he got the sack. Have you any idea how many people are on the dole? Your rotten *Exchange and Echo* was the only job he could get.'

'My dad wouldn't do it. Not if he wrote the truth and they printed lies.'

'Yes, well. We can't all be Clifford Ramsden's daughter, can we?'

She felt the warmth of pride in her cheeks. She could almost bring herself to forgive him for saying that. It was strange to find herself feeling sorry for the Crabtrees. She stared out of the window, wrestling with the last of her anger.

'Well, are you going?' Denis tapped the leaflet in front of him. 'Since you're so keen on people standing up for what's right.'

The old jealousy burned in her that he could even think of asking such a question. He might go, but he must know she couldn't.

'Are you?' she asked warily.

'I'd love to!'

'Well, you know I can't. Mum and Dad would never let me. Not on a Sunday, especially if there might be a fight.'

'Don't be daft. Nor would mine. There was a big enough row last Sunday when I got home late, and a worse one when they found out what I'd been doing. And my dad says there's bound to be trouble on this trespass. The landowners will try everything they can to stop them getting on Kinder Scout. So there's no point in *asking* them if I can go.'

He gave her a long, slow wink.

'What . . .?'

'Ssh!'

Mrs Crabtree came out of the compartment behind them, leaving the door open. She had been joking with Edith's father as though they were still good friends.

'It looks as if the sky's going to clear for us,' she said, as she squeezed past them down the packed corridor.

Edie looked round quickly. Clifford was watching her from just inside the door. She smiled at him and turned back to Denis. That wink must have meant something. But he was gazing innocently out of the window now.

The train rumbled on, climbing through grey-green fields. Beside the sooty sheep there were newborn lambs, startlingly white. Every spring there was this shock, reminding you of the colour sheep were meant to be. How far did you have to climb to escape from the grime of towns and chimneys, till even the leaves and grass were not filmed with black? To the top of Kinder Scout?

They did not talk again until the train had unloaded them at a wayside station in the dales. Edie caught up with Denis in a stone-walled lane under the gold of budding oak leaves.

'What did you mean just now? When you were talking about the trespass and you winked at me?'

He looked round cautiously and spoke in a low voice.

'My mum's got a bike in the shed. It's quite a good one, really, if only she was better with a spanner. Bits have a habit of dropping off it. But I bet I could ride it to the rally at Hayfield, if it didn't fall to pieces on the way.'

'My dad's got a bike! But he never rides it.' The words were out before she knew she was going to say them. Now her thoughts were running away with her, as though they, too, were on a bike and it was going out of control down a steep hill.

He turned to her. His eyes were bright with enthusiasm behind his glasses. Then he frowned.

'But your dad's going to be there himself, isn't he?'

She gave a gasp of relief. 'Yes. And he'd see me, wouldn't he? He'd be bound to send me home.'

They walked on in silence. Then Denis sighed.

'All the same. Just think of it. It could be the most exciting thing we ever get the chance to do. The game-keepers with sticks, the police in Black Marias, trying to stop hundreds of ramblers trespassing. It's just what Nonny said we should do. Claim our right to walk on the mountains.'

Edie laughed. 'My dad says the landowners would like to rewrite the Bible. We ought to say, *I will lift up mine eyes unto the hills . . . if I can get a permit*!'

She began to sing.

'*It's the same the 'ole world over.*
It's the poor wot gets the blame.
It's the rich wot gets the gravy.
Ain't it all a blooming shame!'

They started to giggle. Nonny, suddenly more cheerful than Edie had seen him for weeks, looked over his shoulder and grinned at them.

'Teach me that,' said Denis.

They were still singing when they came round a bend in the lane, and there it was. A vast block of moorland, looming over them, forbidding under lowering cloud.

'Kinder Scout,' Edie murmured. 'The Dark Peak. It's always *there*. Even when I come out of school, I can't help seeing it now above everything else. And I'll never be allowed to stand on the summit.'

'You can,' Denis said. 'There's your dad's bike.'

Chapter 19

'I want to come too.'

Edie ran out of the bedroom. Bobby was standing at th top of the stairs, clutching his stout school shoes in his hand He was still in his pyjama trousers. His mouth trembled a he looked down at his father.

'It's not fair. You always take Edie. It's my tur today.'

The shock of it took Edie's breath away. This day ha been written on her mind in scarlet letters. Sunday, Apri 24th, 1932. The day of the Kinder Scout Trespass. Sh would have given anything to be going with her father, saf beside him. But he would not take her. And here wa Bobby asking to go. *Bobby*!

'You cheeky little thing!' she cried. 'If he takes anyone it'll be me.'

She looked down pleadingly at her father. He wa standing in the hall in his corduroy breeches and flanne shirt. His bulging rucksack was already strapped an waiting. He shook his head gravely. They had been ove this many times before.

Maggie appeared from the kitchen.

'You get your Sunday clothes on, both of you. I know I'l not change your father's mind once he's set on something But there's neither of you going, and that's flat.'

Clifford laid an arm across Maggie's shoulders and kisse her.

'She's right. It's men's work today. They'll have th police out, and all, I shouldn't wonder.'

Maggie sniffed. 'Men! There'll be some hussies as well, from what you say.'

'Aye. Lil, and a few more like her. Tell you what! I'll take you, too, Maggie, if you'd like to come!'

'Get away! I've got better things to do on a Sunday, even if you haven't. And you mind what you get up to. This is a respectable house. I don't want the police coming knocking on my door, telling me you've been arrested.'

'Don't you fret. I'm not going to do anything silly. Just walk to the top of a mountain and down again.'

They hugged each other. Then he stepped out into the yard and drew a deep breath, looking up beyond the grimy stone walls.

'Aye! This is going to be a marvellous day.'

They listened to the swing of his hobnailed boots going up the alley, sounding louder than usual in the Sunday calm.

Then, 'It's not fair!' shouted Bobby, and started to cry.

Edie went quickly back into the bedroom and shut the door. Bobby came in and looked at her suspiciously. He was still sniffing.

'What have you got there?'

She whipped the bundle of Saturday clothes behind her back.

'Just some washing.'

It was the first lie. Was this how it happened? Was this what Miss Lancaster meant? Had she taken the first step down the slippery slope that led to hell?

She had rolled her jumper and socks in her tartan skirt. She went towards the bedroom door. Her mother's footsteps were coming up the stairs. She would be going into the front bedroom to change the sheets on the big double bed. Would she call Edie to help her?

Edie's heart was thumping in her chest, with the daring

of what she was about to do. The trespassing, the police, the gamekeepers with guns, they were all too far away. She could not feel frightened of them yet. Her one great fear was of her mother catching her as she escaped from the house.

She slipped out on to the landing.

'Edie!'

She pushed her bundle hastily into a corner.

'Come and give me a hand to turn this mattress.'

They struggled to push the mattress over. Outside, an orange sun was climbing over the rooftops. Would her mother want her to stay and help make the bed?

'Well, don't stand there gawping. I can manage now.'

There was no one downstairs. She had only a few minutes. Her father's bike was kept in the outside lavatory in the yard. In sudden anxiety she looked up at the back bedroom window. She had forgotten about Bobby. What if he looked out and saw her now? But the window was blank and faceless.

With trembling fingers she placed the note she had written on the floor of the lavatory, where the next person to use it would find it. Then she started to drag the big bike from its resting-place. It was much more heavy and awkward than she had imagined. It was difficult even to hold it upright. At one point it fell with a clatter against the lavatory door.

She looked round in growing terror. She realised suddenly that it was not just Bobby who might be watching. All down the next street, the backs of houses looked down into her yard. Anyone there could be watching her struggling with the rusty machine.

The only answer was speed. She must be up that cobbled alley and away before anyone could call out and stop her. But the yard gate was even harder. She was almost crying as she struggled to hold it open and push the bike through.

Outside, there was a worse problem. Try as she would, she could not mount the bike. It was a man's bicycle with a high crossbar. Every time she tried to swing herself into the saddle, the bike fell over. The greasy pedal wrapped itself in the skirt of her Sunday dress and left a big black stain.

Sobbing with distress, she ran to the end of the alley, with the bike bumping beside her.

The main road was wide and quiet. There was no one about. Calmer now, she managed at last to get her leg over the crossbar and wobbled across the road.

Her first stop was her father's allotment, on the other side of the railway line. He had a tiny shed in the corner. Inside, she stripped off the stained green frock and pulled on the familiar jumper and tartan skirt. She unwrapped her hiking boots. She felt better already as she strapped the laces firmly round her ankles.

It had been bad enough smuggling her clothes out. She had not dared to steal food from the larder, and she had no money. She would have to go without dinner. And she had forgotten to bring a mackintosh.

She stepped out of the toolshed and looked up at the sky. The April sun was struggling through the smoke-haze, climbing hour by hour towards the cloudless blue. Her father was right. Up on the hills it would be a clean, sparkling day.

Balancing the bike against the shed, she climbed on again. As she rode down the path there were a few grunted 'Good mornings' from the bent backs of the gardeners, but only the rows of spring cabbages stood up to watch her go by.

She rolled unsteadily to the foot of the hill where Denis was waiting.

Chapter 20

He caught the bike just in time to save her falling into the road. Her arms were trembling with the effort of clutching at the brakes. And the saddle was so high that she could not put her foot down without falling over.

'I think we'd better swap,' grinned Denis. 'I feel like Miss Lancaster on her way to a jumble sale.'

And then she realised what he was offering her. He was standing astride his mother's bike. It was the primly upright kind, with high handlebars and a basket in front. But it was smaller and newer, shining with chrome, and, best of all, it had no crossbar to tangle with her skirt.

'Could I?' She hoisted herself into the saddle and smiled with relief. Then she looked guiltily across at her father's bike.

'I'm afraid it's rusty. He doesn't use it much. He'd rather walk.'

'I'm not surprised. Aren't there any springs in this saddle? Still, at least the brakes work. I'm never sure with my mother. Every time she mends a puncture, she seems to lose another nut. That thing's only held together with will-power.'

But Mrs Crabtree's bike rolled smoothly along the road. Soon they were spinning out into the countryside.

She had escaped from her mother. By now her disobedience would have been discovered. Her note would have been found. The house would be full of righteous anger. Edie knew it was not that her mother did not love her. It was *because* she loved Edie that she wanted to bring ıer up the right way, to keep her from danger. But Maggie Ramsden's loving anger was a fearful thing.

At the end of the day Edie would have to go home and face that wrath. But not yet. She pushed the fear into the back of her mind and shut the door on it.

But now other fears were taking hold of her. She was afraid of cycling.

She tried to make herself think ahead. She was going to face the people with land, the people with money, the people they said working folk could never take on and win. She, Edie Ramsden, was going to strike her little blow for freedom. If only her father did not see her first and send her home.

Denis glanced sideways at her.

'I say. Are you sure you've ridden a bike before?'

'Yes, of course I have!' she said hotly. 'Several times.'

Three, to be precise. Just to the end of the road and back. Freda had had a shiny new three-speed for her birthday. To show it off, she had let the other girls try it, one by one. Three turns each. And then she had taken it back again. She did not dare tell Denis that. He would never have asked her to come if he had known.

Already her calves were beginning to ache furiously, and the rough wool of her skirt was chafing the tops of her legs as they moved up and down against the saddle. The swooping downhill runs terrified her. They would come flying round a bend and there suddenly was a narrow bridge in front of her. Each time she expected to go crashing into the wall and be catapulted into the rushing beck. And then there was the dragging climb up the other side. She found pushing the bike was almost as hard as riding it. When they came to the top of the hill, there was always that panic in her throat when she had to mount again. If Denis had not been with her, she could never have done it. But the fear of his scorn was sharper than the physical fear.

She felt that when they reached Hayfield she would collapse. Yet that was only the beginning. There was still the Trespass. Kinder Scout. The first mountain she had ever climbed to the top. And she would have to do it on legs that were already like trembling jelly. To think that she could have been at home now, walking to chapel, singing the hymns beside her mother, safe.

'*Stop*!' yelled Denis in her ear for the third time. He put out his hand to grab the saddle.

Next moment the bike seemed to buckle under her, and she fell into the road.

Chapter 21

Edie crawled out from under the bike and limped to the side of the road.

'Are you all right?' Denis asked anxiously.

She rubbed her bruised hip and sat down on the grass verge. 'I think so. What happened?'

The front wheel was still spinning. Denis bent over it.

'I don't know whether it was the bike, or the way you ride it. You were wobbling all over the place. I thought the wheel was going to fall off. I tried to shout. But in the end it was you that fell off.'

'Do you know what's the matter with it?'

'It'll be Mum. She had the front wheel off to mend a puncture last week. I bet she hasn't tightened the nuts.'

He took the tool-kit from behind the saddle and exclaimed with annoyance.

'That's just what I mean. Look at that! Puncture repair outfit, tyre levers, everything except a spanner. She's always like that. Has your dad's bike got one?'

But the tattered saddlebag on Clifford's bike was quite empty.

Denis tested the wheel uncertainly. He tried to tighten the nut with his fingers.

'I suppose I could ride it. It's my fault for not checking it before we started. And it can't be far to Hayfield now. Could you manage your father's bike? It may be ancient, but I bet he's looked after it.'

Edie stood up. She felt a bit dizzy and her legs trembled at the knees. The thought of cycling any further appalled her, and climbing on to that high man's bike with its impossible crossbar was more than she could manage. But there was no way out. She couldn't stay here on her own. And home was so far away now that she dared not even think about turning back.

'I'll try,' she started to say, when a shrill whistling made them both turn their heads.

Over the brow of the hill two more bikes came spinning. In front was a boy no bigger than Denis, with his head down. Snatches of song were torn from his lips by the rushing air. He looked up as he neared them, and drew in the brakes to a long skidding halt. The second bike came whooshing down to stop beside him.

'What's up? Do you need any help?'

'Have you got a spanner? I think this wheel's loose.' Denis was trying to sound in command of the situation.

'Let's have a look, shall we?'

The short stranger slipped a rucksack from his back and stepped forward with a quick smile at Edie. Looking into his face, Edie realised with a start that he was not a boy, but a young man. He reached for the spindle nuts with small, capable hands that were criss-crossed with a web of black lines. Edie knew what that meant. He was in work, engineering most likely. The hands were clean, but oil was etched so deeply into the skin that no amount of washing could quite remove it.

He felt the tension on the spindle and replaced the butterfly screws.

'There's nothing much wrong with that.' He stood the bike up and tested it all over. 'But I'll tell you something else. These handlebars are as loose as my old granny's teeth. I wonder you could steer the thing at all.'

For a few moments his deft fingers were busy with the spanners.

'Here. Try that.'

His warm smile gave Edie the courage to find her voice. She eyed the strangers' rucksacks.

'Are you on your way to Hayfield? Are you going on the Trespass, too?'

The young man looked round sharply at his friend.

'Aye. Very likely we shall!'

And the two of them burst out laughing uproariously.

'Up you get.'

She found herself hoisted into the saddle before her mind or muscles had time to protest.

'Thank you very much,' said Denis stiffly, still cross with himself because he had not noticed the handlebars. 'What's your name?'

'Just call me Bunny!' Again that laughter, as though the two shared a huge secret joke. 'And this is Woolfie.'

And with a whoop, the two young men grabbed their rucksacks, vaulted into the saddle, and went bowling on down the hill.

'Follow us!' Bunny called over his shoulder, still laughing.

Before they knew what was happening, Denis and Edie found themselves swept up in the rush of movement and cycling on towards Hayfield in the wake of the two cheerful young men.

'Are you sure you're all right?' Denis asked.

'Yes,' she said, confidently now.

The bike felt so much firmer and steadier beneath her. It only needed a small movement of her hands to steer it where she wanted it to go. Bunny was right; it wasn't her, it was the handlebars, making everything so much harder than it need have been. She was almost enjoying it now, chasing those two tiny figures through the still Sunday morning.

It seemed no time at all before they rounded a bend and Hayfield was in sight, with its dark church tower and small streets climbing steeply out of the valley. There were crowds of people, ramblers with rucksacks, on both sides of the road. Edie felt a sudden panic that she would see her father. She would be sent back before she had even begun the Trespass.

For a moment she thought she had lost Bunny and Woolfie. But suddenly they were in front of her, standing outside a teashop, holding their bikes and talking to a woman in a white apron. The woman pointed round the side of the house and they started to wheel their bikes through the garden gate.

Bunny waved to Denis and Edie. 'It's all right. You can leave yours here too. They'll be out of sight.'

And then he was off into the teashop, followed by Woolfie, leaving them to stack their bikes beside his in the yard.

Denis stepped over the threshold into the shop. But Edie still stood on the pavement.

'Come on! I'm dying of thirst.'

She reddened. 'I haven't got any money.'

'I'll treat you. I can manage lemonade and sticky buns.'

Still she hesitated. What would her mother say if she accepted money from him? If only she had remembered to bring some dinner.

Then, down the street, she caught a glimpse of ginger hair.

'All right!' she gasped, and scuttled into the teashop.

She should have sat down at once with her back to the window. But she couldn't resist the awful temptation to peer out. She gave a sigh of relief. It wasn't her father's tousled head going past. The crowds were all younger men and women. Inside the teashop a group of them were gathered round a table in the corner, talking excitedly. They seemed to be studying a map. Bunny had almost disappeared from sight in the middle of them. But they could hear his quick, light voice doing much of the talking.

The two children found a table away from the window and sat sipping fizzy lemonade. Edie kept glancing nervously round. Suddenly she drew back, hiding her face.

'Was that him?' Denis asked, watching her.

She nodded. It was silly to feel so frightened, when she had known that her father would be here.

'You realise our parents may have telephoned Hayfield as soon as they realised where we'd gone? Suppose the police are watching out for us already?'

She stared at him in horror. She had not thought about telephones. They had never formed part of her world.

Denis peeped round the curtain.

'It's OK. The coast seems to be clear. Let's slip across to the recreation ground. That's where the rally's supposed to start. There's bound to be somewhere where we can watch without anyone spotting us.'

They were not the only ones to slip out of the teashop unobserved. Bunny and Woolfie were just behind them. The two young men looked warily round them. Then they made off swiftly, not to the meeting-place but towards the hills.

As they crossed the road, Edie seemed to be smaller than anyone else on the streets. She felt that everyone must be staring at her in her hiking clothes. The children of Hayfield would all be indoors, at their Sunday dinners. The people who lived here were keeping out of trouble. Their doors were shut against the strangers on their pavements.

The folk who were gathering outside were a different breed. They were mostly young men and women, bare-kneed in colourful clothes, their faces alive with a nervous excitement, and talking loudly, full of their own daring. It was a strange Sunday.

'There's a lot more police about now,' Denis said anxiously. 'Come on. We'd better find a place to hide.'

Chapter 22

'I don't like it down here,' Denis complained. 'It's like being in a dungeon.'

Edie knew what he meant. They were squatting on damp earth behind a laurel bush. On the other side of it, the ramblers were massing on the green grass of the recreation ground, at the valley bottom. Steep slopes rose up on either side. From above, dark houses frowned down on the Trespassers disapprovingly. She could not even see Kinder Scout from here. She was beginning to feel trapped.

'There's Red Grouse,' hissed Denis. 'But I can't see Bunny or Woolfie. I wonder why they cleared off like that? If they're not back soon, they'll miss the rally.'

'I've never seen so many policemen in my life,' Edie whispered back.

On the road above, a line of black police cars stood parked. There was one big van with barred windows, the Black Maria. Policemen stood by the railings, looking down. There were more of them moving slowly across the field. Against the ramblers' colourful shirts and khaki shorts, their high-buttoned tunics and dark helmets stood out like crows in a flock of bright pigeons.

The children were not completely hidden. Anyone could see them behind the bushes if they looked closely enough. Nonny and Clifford were coming nearer.

'Where's this Benny Rothman?' Nonny called to Lil. 'He's supposed to be organising this, isn't he? If we don't move soon, they'll have us penned here like sheep. We'll never even get near Kinder Scout.'

'Benny'll be here. You'll see,' Lil laughed at him, pushing the curly hair back from her face.

The crowd was growing all the time, chattering in high, excited voices. Edie felt herself caught up in the tension. She knew this feeling: the bright eyes, the raised voices, the too-loud laughter. It was the way she felt in the schoolroom before she went into chapel for the Sunday School Anniversary, to sing in front of the whole church. Or in the front room on election night, as they waited for the runners to come back with the results. The same high hope of success and the sick fear of failure.

'Come on, Red Grouse! Let's have you all in a line,' yelled Lil. 'No. Further apart. Right, bend over!'

In the midday sunshine, the boys and girls spread themselves out across the field. For a moment, Edie couldn't understand what they were doing. Then she saw them bending over, their backs arched, hands resting on their knees, and she began to giggle.

Lil stepped back from the beginning of the line and spat on her hands. The rest of the ramblers drew back, laughing and cheering.

'Come on, Lil! Let's see you clear the lot!'

Edie looked enviously at the older girl with the close-cropped curly hair, in her grey flannel shorts and strong boots. She saw her father smiling as he watched. He must have been the oldest person there, except for the policemen.

Lil took a hop and a spring and came flying down the line, leapfrogging the bent backs. The yells of encouragement grew louder as she cleared one after another. Clifford was cheering with all the rest.

She had almost reached the last doubled figure of Nonny, when a police officer stepped forward right across her path. Lil cut short her leap, stumbled and cannoned into Nonny. The two of them went sprawling on to the ground. Lil was first on her feet. She rounded on the policeman indignantly.

'What did you have to go and do that for? I only had one more to clear.' She rubbed at the angry red bruise on her arm. 'Lucky for you, I didn't break a bone.'

The police officer shook his head. 'I can't allow it. Disorderly behaviour in a public place. It is my duty to require all persons present to conduct themselves in a proper manner.'

The rest of Red Grouse had gathered round him. Their mouths fell open in astonishment. Clifford strolled slowly across to listen.

Nonny burst out, 'Get away! What's a recreation ground for, if it's not for playing games? It's a people's park, not a cemetery!'

The police officer cleared his throat and looked around. Edie snatched her bright skirt further out of sight. A police inspector had stopped just in front of the laurel bush. More policemen began to close in around Red Grouse. All the other ramblers had stopped talking and stood watching.

'No meetings allowed on this field. There's other people, besides you, want to use it. Little kids come here with their mothers on a Sunday afternoon. Hayfield people. You're keeping them off. You don't have permission for what you're doing.'

'Since when did you have to have a permit to play leapfrog?' Nonny shouted.

'Oh, no, Nonny!' Edie whispered. 'Please! Not now!'

Clifford caught his arm. 'Steady, Nonny. We came here to tackle bigger things than this.'

She saw Nonny draw a deep breath. He twisted round and looked high above the treetops to where she knew he would glimpse the dark summit of Kinder Scout. He allowed Clifford to lead him away into the crowd.

Denis let out a sigh of relief too. They dared not move. The police inspector was still standing just in front of the bushes. A constable came running across the grass and saluted.

'Sir! Message from the railway station.'

The inspector sprang to life. 'Bernard Rothman! They've arrested him?'

'No, sir. Sorry, sir. He wasn't on that train either. And there's not another one before two o'clock. And he's not been seen on any of the buses.'

'Then where the devil has he got to? There's no other way he could come from Manchester. Don't tell me he's called this Trespass and now he's not going to turn up to lead it.'

'Perhaps he's funked it, sir. Probably sitting at home with his feet up.'

Someone came across and murmured in Lil's ear. She nudged Nonny and whispered to the rest of Red Grouse. They began to saunter over the grass to the far gate. All round them the field was quietly emptying, the streets clearing. The tide of ramblers was ebbing swiftly and silently towards the steps and the hill that led out of the town to the moors. Behind them they left the policemen, like black rocks uncovered on a beach.

Denis and Edie scrambled to their feet.

'They're all going!' exclaimed Denis. 'They're not going to have a rally here, after all.'

'What shall we do?' cried Edie in sudden panic. Already the field was almost deserted. The startled policemen looked round for orders.

'You! And you! After them!' barked the inspector to six of them. 'The rest of you, get the cars. Head them off on the road!'

The policemen scattered, some following the ramblers, some running for the lines of black vehicles parked on the road above the opposite side of the field.

'Come on!' cried Denis. 'Run!'

They raced across the emptying, lonely grass.

'Hey! You children! Stop! Come back!'

But they did not stop running till they were squeezed in behind the safety of rucksacks and boots as the last of the ramblers shouldered their way up the narrow steps to the road. They looked nervously back. There were policemen following them. The children burrowed deeper into the crowd.

The street was hardly wide enough for a car. The ramblers filled it from wall to wall as they moved steadily uphill in a solid body. Those at the back could not see the leaders. But Clifford's ginger head stood out above the crowd. Edie silently begged him not to turn round.

There was a growling behind them. The police cars were creeping up the hill in low gear. But they had come too late. They could not get past the packed crowd to reach the leaders.

'Clever,' said Denis. 'If they'd had the rally down there, like they'd planned, the Trespass would never even have got started. All the leaders would have been arrested. That Bernard Rothman they keep talking about . . . if he's here.'

'Will they arrest us?' Edie asked, glancing uneasily over her shoulder.

The children were still near the back of the crowd. Behind, there was only a short space between them and the bonnets of the police cars. Six grim-faced policemen were walking beside them. Edie willed herself not to look round again. She fixed her eyes on the canvas rucksack in front of her.

But other heads kept turning, to see what was happening. The rucksack in front of Edie swung round. A cheerful face appeared, fringed with curly hair. There was a moment's puzzlement as the older girl stared down at Edie.

Then, 'Why, you're Clifford's girl, aren't you?' exclaimed Lil. 'Edie Ramsden! However did you get here?'

'Oh, hush!' begged Edie, with her finger to her lips. 'He'll hear you.'

Lil pealed with laughter. 'What? You mean your dad doesn't know you've come on the Trespass? And you as well, Denis? I thought you'd have scuppered your chances last week.'

'Oh, you're not going to tell him, are you? You can't let him send me back now!'

'Why, you little monkey, Edie Ramsden!' cried Lil. 'We'll have you both in the Revolution yet!'

Beside her father, a dark head turned at her name. Edie caught her breath. But Nonny gave her a long, slow wink and put his finger to his lips.

Chapter 23

There was a sudden cheer in front. The march halted abruptly.

'What's happening?' Edie stood on tiptoe, trying to see.

Then, magically, the crowd thinned out in front of her as the ramblers broke into a run. The road had turned into a narrow alley. It was not even wide enough for a single police car. The ramblers were storming up it and pouring out on to the high road that led from the valley. Below, the pursuing cars had ground to a halt, their exhausts fuming. Denis and Edie scrambled out on to the road with all the others.

They swung along now at a fast pace. Beyond the trees that fringed the valley, the great bulk of the open moors was coming nearer. Edie felt a tightness in her throat as she looked up at the summit. Was she really going up there?

Suddenly they found themselves turning off the road into a quarry, already packed with people.

'Quick, behind those stones,' said Denis.

They slipped into a hiding place from which they could listen. They heard the crunch of boots on gravel as someone else came and stood behind them. Edie peeped round. There were two men there, wearing the tweed breeches called 'plus fours'. They did not look like the other ramblers.

Two young men were scrambling up on to a platform of rock. A sea of eager faces turned up to watch them. One of the small figures stepped forward to the edge.

'It's Bunny!' gasped Edie. 'The one who mended my bike.'

'Ssh!'

'You won't all know me, but you'll know the name. I'm Benny Rothman,' he called out to them. 'The chap that should have been giving this speech doesn't seem to have got here, so you can have a few minutes to get your breath back, whilst I use up mine telling you why we're here . . .'

'*He's* Benny Rothman!' said Denis. 'But that's the one who organised all this. The one they were waiting to arrest at the railway station.'

' . . . The police would have stopped me leaving Manchester if they could. But they never thought I'd cycle here.'

'So did we!' whispered Edie proudly.

' . . . You all know the history. The landowners put walls round the common lands that used to belong to everyone. Then they took up shooting grouse, so they stopped us even from walking on the open moors. Every time someone brings up a Bill in Parliament to give us back the right to the mountains, they vote it down. So it's up to us now. Today we're going to take back something that should have belonged to us from the day we were born. And we're going to do it peacefully. We're not going to hurt anyone or damage anything. We don't want to fight them for it. All we want to do is to climb to the top of that mountain. If they catch some of us, there are hundreds more of you to take our places. We're going to stand on the summit of Kinder Scout like free men and women.'

A great cheer rang from the throats of the Trespassers and thundered round the quarry. Edie found she was shouting too. She could see Nonny, waving his cap in the air, beside Clifford.

There was a lump in Edie's throat as she watched her father standing tall above the rest. She knew they were different from the others. She, because she was the youngest person there. He, because he was older than any of them. They were Ramsdens. They hadn't come here to be like other people, but because of what they believed in.

'But don't think they'll let us get by easily. You've given most of the uniformed police the slip. But they've got their spies, even here. Take a good look round you. Those gentlemen near the back in the trilby hats. They'll be Water Board officials. Yes, you, sir. Good afternoon!

'Well, we've no quarrel with them. We're not going to harm their reservoir. The ones you want to watch out for are the plain-clothes detectives. You can pick them out a mile off. They're the ones in plus fours, trying to look like ramblers. But they wouldn't fool my granny's canary. There's two of them over there.'

Edie and Denis ducked down behind the rocks as every face in the quarry swung round in their direction. Edie looked over her shoulder. The faces of the two men behind her had turned bright red. The quarry rocked with laughter.

'What do we do? Arrest him now for incitement to riot?' one of them muttered.

The other shook his head. 'Best not. There's too many of them. Wait till the uniformed boys get here.'

'They'll be gone by then.'

'Don't worry. What goes up must come down. They'll find half the police in Derbyshire waiting for them at the bottom.'

Denis gasped and turned pale. Edie caught his eye. She wondered if she looked as frightened as he did.

Benny Rothman was speaking to them more seriously again.

'And that's not all. Woolfie Winnick and I have been scouting ahead. That's why you haven't seen us till now. Up on that hill, they've got every estate worker in the county waiting for us. They're armed with sticks, or worse. So watch yourselves. But we've got numbers and speed.

'Now, Woolfie Winnick's going to lead. That's him down there with the whistle round his neck. Listen for the signals. One blast means "Advance in open order". Two means "Halt". When you hear him blow three times, that's when you leave the footpath and go straight for the summit of Kinder Scout. They may stop some of us. But they'll never stop us all. Good luck!'

To a great burst of clapping and cheering he leaped down from his platform. At once a small group of friends closed round him, like a bodyguard. The whistle blew one long shrill blast. Edie and Denis slipped out of hiding and dived into the crowd. With Woolfie at their head, the Trespassers poured out on to the road and headed for the heart of the hills and Kinder Scout.

Edie looked round. The men in plus fours were coming after them.

Chapter 24

They were walking along the wall of Kinder Reservoir. A stout man in a flat cap stood and watched them go past in double file. He grasped a stick in his hand, and a golden labrador crouched at his feet. A little wind ruffled the grey-blue surface of the water.

'Nice day for a swim!' Lil called out to him with a cheery smile.

The dog growled. The man gazed straight in front of him, expressionless. Several more of the ramblers wished him a cheerful good-day as they passed, but he did not answer.

'Water Board official,' whispered Denis. 'He's making sure we don't pollute his reservoir.'

Kinder Scout loomed suddenly across the end of the reservoir. Edie made herself lift her eyes and face it. Close to, it was every bit as awesome as she had imagined. There were no easy slopes, no gentle foothills. From here, a wall of grass rose sheer into the sky, towering over them. Its summit seemed to have been ruled flat, massive and horizontal as a giant's billiard table. Just looking up at it sent a stab of weakness through her legs and lungs. Could she really climb that?

A little cloud wandered along the skyline. Once you were up there, once you reached that ridge, you must be able to walk for miles along the summit. With all the world spread out below you. Manchester on one side, Sheffield on the other. Derbyshire, Cheshire, Lancashire, Yorkshire. Millions of tiny houses full of people who had never climbed so high.

The valley was narrowing in front of them. A tiny beck carved its way over stones. The hills closed in around them, walls of heather on either side, shutting out the summit of Kinder Scout. The breeze that had stirred the reservoir could not find them here, and the sun beat into the clough, still and hot.

They were walking in single file now, up the narrow path. From in front came the faint strains of *The Manchester Rambler*.

'*He called me a louse and said "Think of the grouse".*
Well, I thought but I still couldn't see
Why old Kinder Scout and the moors round about
Couldn't take both the poor grouse and me.
He said, "All this land is my master's."
At that I stood shaking my head.
No man has the right to own mountains
Any more than the deep ocean bed.

I'm a rambler, I'm a rambler, from Manchester way.
I get all my pleasure the hard, moorland way.
I may be a wage-slave on Monday,
But I am a free man on Sunday.'

By the final chorus, they were growing breathless. Heads were beginning to turn sideways, scanning the slopes above them. The whistle blew twice.

'What's the hold-up?' asked Denis, as Edie halted suddenly in front of him.

'I can't see.'

Edie looked round warily for her father. At every stile and halt, when the mass of the ramblers waited for each other, she had been afraid that he would catch sight of her as she scrambled over or sat down for a rest. It was Nonny who saved her. Just as her father turned towards her, Nonny caught his attention and drew it away to the mountain in front of him. She subsided with relief on to a cushion of heather and scooped palmfuls of cold water into her mouth.

Then they were moving again. She made herself watch Lil's boots in front of her, not thinking of anything but the next step.

Suddenly there were three blasts from the whistle up ahead. A great shout rang down the line like a war-cry. The Trespassers broke from the path and flung themselves on the slopes. They were using hands as well as boots, hauling themselves up through the heather, scrambling, half-running, pouring over the moor in a surging line of colour.

Edie forgot the ache in her calves in the terror of being left behind. There was a burning pain in her lungs as she gasped for breath. But her feet were sending her body shooting upwards with a strength she had not known she had. Her eyes were still fixed on Lil's red socks, going ever further ahead. She had lost sight of Denis.

Then she heard his voice quite close on her right.

'Edie! Look out!'

She lifted her eyes. Above her, Lil had halted abruptly. Across the skyline stood a row of men. With their backs to the afternoon sun they were black silhouettes. Edie could not see if the black things they carried were sticks or guns. There must have been a dozen of them. They came marching down the hill towards the Trespassers, slow and sure. Tramp, tramp, tramp came their boots through the heather. Against the bright sky, she could not read their faces.

'Dodge!' cried Denis. 'We've got to get past them!'

Above them, Lil was already running to her right. Edie did the same. But an outcrop of rock barred her way. The keepers were coming nearer. The children doubled back like rabbits, Denis sprinting ahead, showers of black peat flying back from his boots, Edie's tartan skirt catching in the heather. The last of the Sunday curls were flopping into her eyes. Suddenly the toe of her boot caught in a rabbit-hole, and with a cry of anguish she fell face downward.

Denis turned, hesitated for a moment, and came running back. But high above, someone else had heard her.

Nonny's shout came ringing down the hillside.

'*Edie*!'

She lifted her head. She saw a keeper break from the end of the line and come charging towards her. He was brandishing his stick against the sky.

Nonny leaped down the slope, bellowing furiously.

'Drop that!'

She could not scramble to her feet fast enough.

The keeper reached her first. Nonny flung himself down from the rock above. He grasped the keeper's stick from behind. The man was spun round. Against the dazzle of sunlit sky, the two of them toppled backwards and forwards as they grappled for possession of the stick.

Clifford was dashing downhill with long, flying strides. He was calling out, 'Give over, Nonny! He'd never hit the child! Don't be daft!'

He flung himself between them, forcing Nonny away from the gamekeeper. Nonny grabbed for the stick again. The keeper tugged at it. But his hands slid from the polished wood and his body, suddenly released, tumbled backwards. As he fell, his head hit a small outcrop of stone. He lay on his back, his eyes closed. A small trickle of blood crept down into his hair.

Denis helped Edie to her feet and the two of them stared down at the fallen keeper. Still panting, Nonny let the stick drop. He looked scared. Clifford was already on his knees, bending over the man.

'Are you all right, lad?'

There was a small silence. The man's face was very white. Then he opened hard, bright eyes. He stared up into Clifford's face with hatred.

'I'll get you for this. By heaven, I will. I never forget a face.'

Nonny was struggling to get his breath back. 'You've got it all wrong! It wasn't Clifford. It was me.'

'Never mind about that for now,' said Clifford. 'Are you badly hurt? Shall I fetch you a drink of water?'

The keeper sat up.

'I'll see you in hell first,' he swore.

He stumbled to his feet and put his hand to his head. The blood was still dripping. The other keepers had disappeared down the hill. There were angry shouts rising from below. He looked round at all the watching Trespassers.

'You've not heard the last of this, by a long way.'

'Then look at me! I'm the one who was fighting you,' Nonny protested.

'I know what I saw.' The keeper stared venomously at Clifford. 'And I'll make him pay.'

He limped off down the hill.

Edie made herself look up. Her father was standing over her, unsmiling.

Chapter 25

Clifford's blue eyes stared down at Edie.

'Oh, aye? And does your mother know you're here?'

'I left a note.'

She lifted her eyes to meet his, trying to see how angry he was. But she could not read his expression.

'You . . . left . . . your . . . mother . . . a . . . note . . .'

Her gaze fell before his.

'And what about you?' He turned to Denis. 'Does anyone know you're here?'

'I didn't say anything,' Denis muttered. 'But they'll have guessed where I've gone.'

There was a grim pause.

'I'm sorry!' Edie whispered.

'Aye, and I'll tell you something else for free. You'll be a whole lot sorrier when you get home and face her. And don't look to me to talk her round. I'll have some explaining to do on my own account now, by the sound of it.'

'But it was Nonny who fought him! You tried to stop them!'

He shook his head. 'Once you put your hand to something like this, there's no "me" and "thee". We're all in it together. I knew what could happen. And so did your mother. That's why she didn't want me to come.'

'Or me,' Edie said in a low voice.

He laid his hand on her shoulder.

'I see you're learning.'

They walked on together, with Nonny ahead of them,

silent now. The keepers had all disappeared. The shouting was hushed. Above, there was only the long line of Trespassers all working their way towards the summit.

Suddenly a figure rose out of the heather in front of them. Lil stood barring their way. She raised one finger to her lips. Her other hand pointed at the ground.

'Ssh! And you watch where you're putting your big feet, Clifford Ramsden.'

Their eyes followed her pointing finger to a hollow in the heather. The soft cup of earth was alive with frantic movement. Six bulging heads craned upwards from downy bodies. Six yellow beaks gaped at the sky.

'So that's what it's all about?' Clifford said softly.

'The red grouse. Just a handful of beak and feathers that'll be somebody's dinner on Her Grace's table come August. Poor little beggars!' He lifted his eyes and looked sadly at the summit. 'And for *that*, they deny us the freedom to climb the mountains!'

Edie gazed at the hungry nestlings, fascinated. Then she swung round and saw all the blue valleys below her. She had no breath to speak.

'I'm going to take a bit of eggshell, for a keepsake.' Denis reached forward towards the nest.

Lil smacked his hand away.

'Get off! Don't you dare touch that nest! Do you want the parents to desert the chicks?'

Denis reddened. He murmured, 'I'm sorry. I didn't think.' His voice sounded humble and apologetic.

Edie flashed him a look of sympathy. Her eyes begged him not to be angry again. He musn't let it spoil the friendship between them this time. Not today.

He gave her back a rueful smile. It made him look younger. He didn't seem so much like a clever grammar-school boy now. More like Bobby really.

They left Lil behind, standing sentinel over the nest.

They had their heads down, toiling up the last and steepest slope, when there was a cry of alarm from above. The scattered line of Red Grouse looked up, startled. Ranks of black figures stretched along the skyline. There were scores of them, waiting on the summit for the Trespassers.

'They've beaten us, after all!' Nonny cried bitterly. 'I thought we'd got past that lot too easily. We should have known they'd have reinforcements waiting to stop us getting anywhere near the top.'

Clifford looked longingly up at the summit. Then he turned slowly and took in the view behind him. He gave a long sigh.

'Well, it's been a grand day, all the same. We've had a fair old climb. Though it's not been quite my idea of a Sunday ramble. Speaking for myself, I come into the hills for a bit of peace and quiet, not a stand-up scrap.' Nonny looked away. 'All the same, I'd dearly have loved to stand on that summit today.'

'Hey! What's happening?' cried Nonny. 'Are they going to make a fight for it?'

The leading Trespassers had broken into a run, not back but forwards. They were making straight for the waiting figures on the skyline. The two ranks closed and seemed to grapple. Then, as the advancing silhouettes turned, their rucksacks were clearly seen. Their hands were outstretched to greet the newcomers. The two groups were slapping each other on the back.

'They're ours!' shouted Nonny, racing forward. 'It's the lot from Sheffield! They've come up from the other side. We've won! We're through to the top!'

They all stormed up the last slope, on to the ridge, and were embraced into the welcoming crowd. Nonny whirled Clifford round.

'We've made it! I told you we would! We've conquered Kinder Scout!'

'Nay, lad,' Clifford told him, shaking him gently off. 'Don't talk daft. There's no one can conquer a mountain. You've only climbed it.'

Yet there was a deep smile of joy on his face as he turned away.

Edie was embarrassed to find Denis grasping her hand and shaking it hard.

'We did it!' he panted.

Then she looked around. Everywhere people were shaking hands, clapping each other on the back, hugging. She squeezed Denis's hand and burst out laughing with happiness.

'Yes, we really did!'

She collapsed on to a rock.

Denis lowered himself wearily beside her. To her surprise he looked worse than she felt. He was pale and still struggling for breath.

Nonny ran up to them, still shining with excitement. He held out a bar of chocolate.

'Well done, little 'uns! Here, catch!'

Denis turned pink with pleasure.

The crowd was moving past them. Edie let them go. The sunshine soaked into her, warming her soul. She had done it. She had climbed her mountain. She was here on the summit of Kinder Scout. All around her there was laughter and chatter. But just beyond the edge hung a blue veil of silence.

She pointed downwards.

'That must be Mermaid's Pool.'

A tiny tarn, like a diamond, lay just below them. Beyond, the gleam of the reservoir at the foot of the valley. And after that, mile upon mile of stillness spread across the Sunday countryside.

From far away a single church bell began to chime, calling the local children to Sunday School. It spoke to that part of Edie that should have been in Oldway Chapel now. What was it her father had told her? Chapel had made him the man he was. Then it would make her like him, she promised herself. She would be back there next week. But for this one Sunday she was here, now. On the summit of Kinder Scout. And she would always remember this day.

A skylark rose above her head. She tried to follow it upwards. But it soared on and on into the blue, further than any eye could hold it. From the skies, its song came tumbling down around them.

Chapter 26

'You all know what to do.' Benny Rothman finished addressing the victory rally on the summit of Kinder Scout. 'We're not going to run away. We're not going to pretend we weren't here. We know they're waiting for us down there. They'll be barring the roads and the railway stations. Well, we'll show them we're not ashamed. What have we done? We've spent Sunday on top of a mountain. Let them put us in prison for that, if they dare!'

His smile reached out to include all of them, even Edie.

They came down from the mountain shoulder to shoulder, singing, with Benny Rothman at their head.

But an uneasy silence fell over them as they neared the road. There was always this sense of loss, when their boots left the soft crunch of peat and gravel, and they came back to the tarmac and the town and the smoke, and Monday loomed ahead again.

But today it was worse. A line of black police cars was parked beside the road, with the Black Maria. Grim-faced policemen barred the highway. There was a knot of gamekeepers, and the detectives who had followed the Trespass. Beside the van, one young man, clutching a bundle of newspapers, was already under arrest.

Clifford looked round for Edie and squeezed her hand reassuringly.

'Chin up. No need to look like a wet weekend. They gave over transporting convicts to Australia a while back.'

'He's here,' muttered Nonny. 'The chap who went for Edie.'

They could pick out the gamekeeper clearly. He had a large patch of sticking-plaster on the side of his head. He was watching the ramblers as they came through the gate.

Edie squeezed through after her father. She took her hand from the wall. It was filmed with soot again. She was down from the hills.

The ramblers waited silently. One of the detectives who had stood behind Edie in the quarry started to walk down the line. There were uniformed policemen on either side of him.

He came straight to Benny Rothman and pointed at him.

'I want him, for a start.'

Edie watched miserably as a policeman took Bunny by the arm and arrested him. The detective came on past the ranks of Trespassers, his eyes searching their faces keenly. Every so often his hand touched another sleeve.

'And I'll have him . . . and him . . . and him . . . and him.'

They led four more Trespassers away to the Black Maria.

The detective was coming nearer. He studied Clifford's face and then Nonny's, and his eyes moved on to the end of the line. He nodded, and turned away satisfied. Edie went limp with relief.

But the gamekeeper stepped forward and grasped the nearest policeman by the elbow. His finger stabbed at Clifford.

'That's him! That's the one that hit me!'

Nonny broke forward with a cry of protest. 'Nobody hit you! You slipped and cut your head on a stone. Clifford was trying to stop a fight!'

But Clifford smiled faintly and shook his head.

'You're wasting your breath, lad. He'll not believe you. It's me he wants.'

Nonny, Edie and Denis stood shocked into silence as

Clifford was marched towards the police van. He twisted his head round with a crooked grin.

'I'm sorry, love. I'd have spoken up for you. Now it's you that's going to have to explain for me. But you can tell your mother this: I wouldn't have taken you willingly today, but I'm proud now there were two Ramsdens on Kinder Scout. This will be a day to remember.'

They pushed him into the Black Maria and the doors clanged shut. The ramblers tried to raise a brave cheer as the van rolled away. Edie swallowed hard.

As soon as the van had gone, the cheering died. The rest of the Trespassers were left at the roadside, disconsolate.

Nonny muttered, 'I should have been in that van, not Clifford.'

Woolfie Winnick tried to raise a smile.

'Me too. I led this Trespass, didn't I? So what happens? Benny gets a free lift back in the Black Maria, and I'm left with two bikes to ride back to Manchester on my own. There's justice for you!'

Nonny still looked shocked.

'You'd better come back on the train with us,' he ordered Edie and Denis.

'Yes!' Edie whispered.

They both knew there was still Margaret Ramsden to face.

They left Denis to make his own explanations.

Edie's courage was at its lowest ebb as they walked slowly down the alley to the back gate. This was the moment she had been dreading all day. As she stepped into the yard the back door flew open and Maggie stood there, hope struggling against worry in her face.

Edie stood still for a long moment, watching first relief and then joy dawn in her mother's eyes. Then Maggie flew across the yard and hugged her tightly.

'Oh, Edie! Thank the Lord you're safe!'

She lifted her gaze past Edie's head, looking for another face. Her eyes met only Nonny's. Maggie went white. She took the burden of explanation from both of them.

'You don't have to tell me!' she said. 'He's got himself arrested.'

Chapter 27

'Call that a fair trial for working folk?' Maggie exclaimed, as she hurried across the town square scattering the pigeons. 'A jury of landowners? For a case of trespass?'

On the grand jury that had committed them for trial there had been two brigadier generals, three colonels, two majors, three captains, two aldermen and eleven country gentlemen.

The policeman on the door hadn't wanted to let Edie in to the Assizes, saying that she was too young. But her mother had said firmly that it was Edith's father in the dock and she had a right to be there. Before Margaret Ramsden's stare the policeman had coughed and shuffled and then let them both in. Looking up at her mother, Edie thought it must be hard to be a grown-up, and have to pretend to be so firm and determined. Inside, Edie knew, her mother had been as worried and frightened as she was about what was going to happen to Edie's dad.

Edie was wearing her Sunday clothes, and it felt like Sunday, sitting on wooden benches just like pews, half-listening to the voices of men in sober black with white wigs, talking on in words too difficult to understand. Her mother had not worn her Sunday coat and hat. Proud Margaret Ramsden might be, but it was not Sunday and the court was not God's house. Her second-best coat and hat would do well enough for men's business. She sat straight-backed beside Edie, her gloved hands clenched on her lap and her mouth tight and disapproving, hiding what she felt inside.

All through the long dull hours of the trial Edie had waited till it should be her father's turn, knowing that once he started to speak the whole courtroom would come to life. She could see him standing tall in the dim sunlight, with his hair flaming and his warm, deep voice ringing round these old, dark walls. She even knew what he would talk about. She could have said it herself. He would tell them about the open air and the climbing hills; about the deep paths, lost in a tangle of grass and brambles; about the beat of rain on his shoulders, and the sheep looming out of the mist; of the cutting edge of the wind and the hot, dry summers; the ache in the knees and heavy boots swinging the legs forward and on, hour after hour; the palmful of water from the beck and the bite of mint cake that kept you going to the top. And on the summit, the whole of Britain, so it seemed, blue and all to be explored, spreading away in every direction to the sparkle of rivers and the last blue barrier of hills before the sky touched earth.

The people in the witness box came and went, as though someone were turning the pages of a picture book. Policeman, landowner, gamekeeper. 'You'll not tell me he still needs sticking-plaster after all this time!' hissed Edie's mother, and glared at the usher who told her to be quiet. She was as much a fighter as her husband, in her own way.

Clifford Ramsden answered their questions quietly but firmly.

There was not a single witness for the accused. Denis was in school. Nonny had begged to come, but Clifford had told him not to be so daft as to risk losing a day's pay and even his job. Others were walking the streets with only the dole in their pockets and no money for the fare to Derby. Besides, not one of the prisoners was ashamed of what they had done.

Only Edie was there. She could have told them what happened. But nobody asked her.

At last, Benny Rothman got to his feet and told the story of how the ramblers had struggled for years for the right to walk on the mountains. Edie watched him, remembering his clever hands mending her bicycle. She glanced at the others beside him, at their young, thin faces. She recognised some of them. She had marched with them out of the quarry to Kinder Scout. But always her eyes came back to her father, waiting for him to speak, waiting for him to make them feel what it was really like to walk the hills.

It was the judge's turn. Then suddenly everyone was standing. Seven men who had challenged the law and stood on top of a mountain were turning and going down into the darkness of the cells. It was all over! She should have told the court. She should have jumped to her feet and shouted it out to the whole world. But she had left it too late. She looked at her mother in horror.

'The jury's considering its verdict,' snapped Maggie Ramsden.

When the jury came back they found six of the ramblers guilty. The judge gave Clifford Ramsden six months for assault and Bernard Rothman four months for incitement to riotous assembly. Four other defendants were given sentences of six months, three months and two months.

So it was true. It was true what they were calling in the playground about Edie's father. He was in prison now. And for what? Edie sat in the darkness of the girls' lavatories and made herself remember.

He was in prison for a climb through the rustling heather, for the feel of the clean Pennine wind in his face; for the view of sunlit counties from the summit, for the sound of the skylark singing over Kinder Scout.

Outside in the playground, the whistle blew for afternoon school. Edie put away her wet hankie, pulled up her knickers and straightened her skirt. She pushed the door and it swung open on to the playground.

The whole school was waiting. The children were lined up in front of the wall, class by class, from the infants to the biggest juniors. Even the teachers turned their heads to look at her.

Edie lifted her chin defiantly and stared over their heads. Over the playground wall, over the roofs, over the smoking chimneys. Away to the massive crest of Kinder Scout. Even in the summer air the haze hung heavy over the cotton mills. But she would not look at that. High on the hills the air would be cloudless blue. She knew because she had been there.

She was a Ramsden. As she marched across the playground towards the lines of staring children she began to sing. Breathlessly at first, then the words came louder and clearer as she remembered her father.

'*I'm a rambler, I'm a rambler from Manchester way.*
I get all my pleasure the hard moorland way.
I may be a wage-slave on Monday.
But I am a free man on Sunday.'

Her father was in prison. But one day the law would change. One day he would stand on the summit of Kinder Scout like a free man. And she would be beside him.

Up there on the mountain, the skylark was still singing for them.